Dangerous Secrets

··

Patricia Fisher Ship's Detective Book 9

Steve Higgs

Contents

Worrying Signs

The police car was a bad sign. It was easy to spot from a long way off and its parked position outside the home of Allen Gibson sent a worrying message. It was not nearly so concerning as the coroner's van parked behind it.

I was returning from a lunch date with Mike Atwell, an old friend who had recently chosen to leave his career in the Kent Police to pursue a new life as a private investigator. He'd taken over my old detective agency. I hadn't exactly planned to abandon it, but the call of globetrotting adventure and the affections of a certain cruise ship captain caused me to leave the country and I was only back in England now because I chased a mystery all the way here.

Driving my car, a vintage Aston Martin, my butler (and best friend in the world) turned his head just a touch to ask, "Should I pull over, madam?"

I pursed my lips. The presence of the police, even outside the home of a person I know, ought not to be any of my business. However, I am known as a sleuth, and though I cannot tell you where the skill, or ability to solve mysteries comes from, I have long since given up denying I possess it.

"Yes, please, Jermaine." I made a snap decision.

I have known Allen for many years for we reside in the same small village tucked into the southeast corner of England where the winters are mild and the countryside is green. For as long as I can remember he has held the position of church treasurer. That's not his job, obviously, it's an unpaid position. Racking my brain to recall his profession, I couldn't recall if it was something in insurance, or banking, though it was definitely money related.

Jermaine glided to the curb and stopped, quickly exiting so that he could open and hold my door for me.

My eyes were yet to leave the front of Allen's house which was why I was looking the right way when two men came out with a body on a stretcher. Not that the body was on display, you understand, but what else could it be? It was clearly heavy, given the strain and perspiration I could see, and unless Allen had been on a crash diet, he wasn't the lightest of men.

Biting down on an upwelling of sadness, I slipped out of my car and told myself not to jump to conclusions. I didn't know for sure that it was Allen.

It was though, I found out two seconds later when Mavis from the post office spotted me.

"You gonna figure out who killed him then?" she asked, crossing the road to get to me.

You might think the presence of the police car was an indication of foul play, but I know the authorities are called to the scene of any unexpected death.

I said, "Hello, Mavis," as a formality, since I hadn't seen her in months, but quickly added, "Is it Allen?"

She nodded, her face showing little emotion. "I heard he was stabbed." Working in the village post office which doubles as the village store, Mavis is the centre of all gossip and knows things no one ought to know about almost everyone. Quite how she might have learned the method of dispatch intrigued me, but not so much as the why.

"Someone stabbed the church treasurer?" I murmured, mostly to myself.

"Old Mrs Forrester said she saw a lady leaving his place late last night. I reckon he had a fancy woman who he lured in with the promise of gifts and holidays – he wasn't short of a penny, I can tell you – but when he failed to deliver, she chose to do him in and make off with whatever cash he had lying about."

While I could not rule out the possibility, other scenarios, literally any of them, sounded more plausible.

The men with the stretcher reached the coroner's van where they began to load the body inside. I watched out of morbid curiosity more than anything else, and in my head I was paying my respects to a man I knew.

However, when a uniformed police officer came close enough to the living room window for me to see who it was, I started walking. Asking Jermaine to pull over and exiting my car, there was never any idea that I was going to involve myself, yet here I was strolling down the garden path toward the front door.

I guess the people inside saw me coming, for I was met at the door.

"Mrs Fisher," Constable Patience Woods acknowledged me. "I didn't realise you were in the area." Patience is a larger-than-life black woman with an attitude to match. I like her.

"I'm keeping a low profile," I replied. At least I had been. Clearly that statement no longer held true. My name, if you haven't figured it out, is Patricia Fisher. Just two days ago I made global headlines when I found the location of an ancient Spanish treasure haul. Taken from mines in the New World three hundred years ago, it was subsequently stolen by the officers of the ship sailing it back to Spain in what the papers were calling 'The World's Greatest Heist'.

I hadn't exactly been looking for it, I was trying to solve a murder, a task at which I succeeded. In the end. However, the treasure find was a bigger story and the press were all over it. And me. And not for the first time.

Getting to the point with Patience, I asked, "Was he murdered?"

Patience didn't answer, not straight away. Instead she ducked her head back inside the house to check who might be listening.

"Is Quinn here?" I guessed.

Patience snorted like a bull. "No, he isn't. Are you crazy? If he caught me talking to you, he would have an aneurism on the spot. I was just checking with Brad. Quinn is on his way, and I don't want him to find you here when he arrives." Holding up a hand to beg a moment's grace, she hollered, "Hey, Brad?"

"Yeah?" echoed back through the house.

"What's the ETA on Quinn?"

"Five minutes. Why?"

Patience beckoned me inside the house. "Okay, we got four minutes. Let's do this quick."

I loved that Patience was so willing to involve me. We have worked together more than once, and she is always the island of sanity in the vortex of madness that so often surrounds her boss. I believe Chief Inspector Quinn started out as a good cop, an honourable man with the best intentions, yet somewhere along the way ambition got the better of him and now he is so consumed with the need to climb the ladder that he cares not who he climbs over or ruins to get there.

I hustled into the house, a quick wave at Jermaine to let him know I was fine and would only be a couple of minutes. Jermaine is far more than my butler, he is my bodyguard too, my chef while we are on the ship, my confidant, and, as I already mentioned, my best friend.

He could see who I was with though, so he probably wasn't too worried about me getting attacked.

Patience led me through Allen's house. This was my first time visiting it, but the layout was familiar and repeated all over the area in similar houses.

"His body was found here," Patience pointed to a spot by the back door. We were in the kitchen where an obvious bloodstain marred the otherwise pristine tile floor. "The murder weapon appears to be a kitchen knife, but not one taken from his knife block."

I looked around until I spotted the selection of knife handles held at forty-five degrees inside a shaped block of wood. They were clearly all there.

"It was still in his body when we got here," Patience let me know.

That was interesting. The knife would be a key piece of evidence if the set it came from could be located.

"Estimated time of death?" I asked. That Allen's body had been taken away told me he'd been dead long enough for the forensics team to get here, do their stuff, and leave having decided there was no more evidence to gather.

"Probably late last night. There are detectives out canvassing the area already."

They would want to know when he was last seen, by whom, and who they saw him with. Many times I have heard it said that the last person to see a person alive is generally the killer. If one chose to be flippant, they could say that was obvious, but what the cliché really means is that the person who admits to having seen them closest to the time of death often proves to be lying about not having stuck them with a knife at the same time.

In a distracted way, I asked, "Anyone I know?"

Patience shook her head. "New people. Detective Sergeant by the name of Alice Prince. She's ok, but she's not someone you want to mess with. She's working with a new guy who's just made it into CID, Detective Andy Sharples. He's not the brightest bulb, which is a little worrying, but he's ok too."

Brad Hardacre stuck his head through the kitchen door. "Might want to make yourself scarce, Mrs Fisher. The chief inspector will be here any minute."

I acknowledged his warning with a nod and started moving. I'm not scared or even phased by Chief Inspector Quinn, but he is an odious man with a narcissistic need to put others down so he can feel superior. I have no need to waste my energy speaking with him.

Leaving via the front door, I was caused to stop when Patience asked, "Will you be looking into this?"

I glanced down the road to see if there were any headlights coming. It was mid-afternoon in early December and the afternoon was fast turning to dusk. Since there were none, I turned to face Patience.

"No, I don't think so. I wasn't planning to stay in England for very long, just a few days until we can rejoin the ship in California."

If I read her expression correctly, this response was not what Patience expected to hear. I get that I am known for solving mysteries, but I have almost always had a reason to do so. Admittedly sometimes that reason was because I might die if I didn't figure out who the killer was, but most recently it has been because I chose to be a paid detective.

The police would find Allen's killer, I had no doubt.

The Promise of Retribution

"Come along, Rex!" Albert called into the darkness. The sun, rather than setting at this time of the year, chose instead to simply fall out of the sky like it had been shot. Were it to exit the day any more dramatically, it would have to be likened to an escaping balloon, whizzing through the air as it deflated.

The day was filled with light when they set off for the park and would have still been so on their return leg, but a squirrel chose to taunt his dog by running across the field, so even though Rex was about as well trained as a dog could be, he was still unable to resist the need to give chase.

That was twenty minutes ago.

Rex didn't catch the squirrel, which reached a tree a few seconds before he was due to get chomped. Albert's dog then found himself facing multiple opponents who gleefully launched acorns from their lofty positions until he got mad enough to try climbing the tree.

Naturally, that didn't work; his body was not designed for such feats.

Responding to his human's voice, Rex had attempted to return to him four times, yet upon each occasion the squirrels or, the squirrel mafia as he preferred to think of them, lured him back with fresh insults. They would shimmy down the tree trunks and twitch their tails. For Rex, for any dog, it was like a trout spotting a lure in the water: utterly irresistible.

"Come on, Rex!" bellowed Albert again. He didn't want to have to wade through the undergrowth to get to his dog, not now that it was so dark and he couldn't see the ground. The likelihood of twisting an ankle was just too high.

Rex narrowed his eyes at the trees. He didn't want to kill the squirrels. He just wanted to hurt them really bad.

An acorn smacked into his skull, this one landing right between his eyes. He barked his frustration, threatening terrible vengeance if he ever got the chance.

"*What this situation needs,*" he remarked to himself, "*is reinforcements.*" At the sound of his human's voice yet again demanding his return, Rex issued a final promise of retribution and slunk back through the bushes to find the old man.

Albert, a long-retired detective superintendent was getting close to his seventy-ninth birthday. He loved his dog, but his tolerance for the cold was no longer what it had been and the chill wind, which hadn't been present when they set off, was making his joints hurt.

"About time, Rex," Albert sighed, grabbing the dog's collar and ruffling the fur around his ears as he clipped the lead in place. "Maybe you don't want your dinner, but I certainly want mine."

"*Dinner?*" Rex's ears pricked up. At the very thought, his stomach rumbled. Many hours had elapsed since breakfast.

It wasn't far back to their house as the crow flies, but the old man took the longer route around the houses and along the paths where lampposts bathed the street with light.

Nearing their house, Rex sensed movement ahead and tensed, his hackles rising automatically. There was someone at their house. For many dogs this would prompt a sense of excitement and happiness, but Rex remembered all too well how many people had tried to hurt his human in recent times. One pair even came to his house, not that they got inside. Instead they sprung an ambush in the street, escaping in their car with Rex giving chase on foot.

Albert didn't notice the visitor waiting in the shadow outside his front door. His mind was elsewhere, his thoughts focussed on his next trip. Inside the house, his bags were mostly packed and just about ready to go.

His passport had required renewal otherwise he might have already left the country. However, when Rex began a low growl emanating from deep inside his chest, he knew to pay attention.

The wind shifted, carrying the scent of their visitor to Rex's nose and he relaxed, his tail twitching with pleasure now that he knew the identity of the stranger at their door.

"*It's Roy*," he chuffed happily.

Close enough now that Albert's neighbour from across the street saw when they passed under a streetlight, Roy raised his hand to wave and called out. A former RAF pilot with combat experience from the Falklands Conflict, Wing Commander (retired) Roy Hope wore a bushy grey moustache, favoured tweed, and carried a slender walking cane that secretly contained a thin sword.

"Pip, pip, old boy. Been out for a walk?"

"Rex needs his exercise," came the honest reply. Albert pulled on the lead, reeling Rex in a little so he could unclip his lead.

Free to go, Rex darted forward, leaping the low wall at the edge of the garden to land on the front lawn. By the time Albert rounded the wall and made it up the short driveway to his door, Rex had performed his standard greeting and was waiting impatiently to get in.

"*Come on, old man. It's dinner time!*"

His rush to get inside meant he missed what Roy had to say. Albert's neighbour needed a second to introduce the topic, which was all the time Albert needed to unlock his door and let Rex in. However, when his right foot twitched to get into the warm, the words he'd just heard Roy say sunk in.

Albert paused on his doorstep, and turned to face his friend.

Repeating the one word that caught his attention, Albert questioned, "Murdered?"

Signs

"Hey, Patty, how was your day?"

The question came from Barbie, one of my dearest friends and a person I have been through more scrapes with than ought to be feasible in one lifetime. She's twenty-two, from California, and has the face and body of a Hollywood actress crossed with a track athlete.

She was currently snuggled into her boyfriend, Hideki, who waved his hand in greeting and paused the TV show they were watching. The pair of them, plus Jermaine, were taking a few days in England to recuperate from our latest adventure.

There were more of us when we arrived, but my assistant, Sam Chalk, grew up in the village, so took the opportunity to go home to be with his parents and pet dog. My security team of six officers from the Aurelia took one look at the miserable weather in England and chose to jet off to California in advance. They would relax on the beach and enjoy the sun until the cruise ship arrived just a couple of days from now.

I considered doing the same, but this is my home and it felt right to stay for a few days. I have a large house on the outskirts of a small village, a gift from the Maharaja of Zangrabar whose impending nuptials I was set to attend in the near future. He insists on the need to be my benefactor, providing me with the house, cars, and what appears to be limitless money all because I saved his country, his throne, and his life.

Looking at it from his point of view I guess I could understand why he wanted to reward me. I was still learning to be comfortable with it.

To reply to Barbie, I said, "My day was lovely ..."

"But?" Anyone could have heard the 'but' at the end of my sentence.

I blew out a tired breath. "But a friend of mine died." I replied, still sifting through my thoughts on the subject.

Barbie rolled away from Hideki, sitting up straight and then standing.

"That's awful, Patty. Is it someone I know?"

I frowned, thinking about whether she would remember Allen. "Maybe. He was the church treasurer, Allen Gibson."

Barbie's face went thoughtful. When I returned to England from my first trip around the planet, both Barbie and Jermaine came with me. For a time I thought we were all going to live here together, but circumstances changed that quickly enough. Nevertheless, we lived in the village for several months and attended the village church where she would have seen Allen even if she never spoke to him.

"Glasses, brown hair, late forties?" she enquired.

I nodded solemnly. "I believe he was murdered."

Barbie's eyes flared at the news and Hideki joined her in standing.

"New case?" he assumed.

I pursed my lips. "I'm not sure. I shouldn't have to investigate, and I wanted to keep a low profile." The papers wanted interviews. The TV people did too. How could I have known solving a few mysteries would have brought such fame? Though perhaps notoriety is a better term.

Barbie came to me, and Hideki crossed the living room to get to the drinks cabinet.

"Gin?" questioned Hideki needlessly. When I nodded, he set out three glasses and began to make drinks.

Barbie gave me a hug.

"If you want to investigate, we will help you. You know that, right?"

We broke the hug to receive our drinks with a word of thanks.

"We are supposed to be flying home in a few days," I replied. Then I realised what my words implied. Most people would say that we were home, but to me, at this point in my life, my real home was a suite on a cruise ship. That was where I felt most centred. My boyfriend, Alistair, the captain of the ship, was there too. As were my pair of miniature dachshunds, Anna and Georgie. Not that I needed to worry about them. If anything, they were likely loving all the additional attention they were getting on the bridge of the cruise ship.

Barbie shot me a sad smile, she was amused by my faux pas, but having just announced the murder of someone I knew, laughter would not be appropriate.

"So, you'll let the police solve the case?" she sought to confirm.

"Can you do that?" asked Hideki. His question hit the nail on the head.

I didn't need to stick my nose in. There was every reason to believe the police would conduct a tight investigation, gathering the facts they needed to find the person behind Allen's murder. However, I couldn't help feeling that the world had dropped this case into my lap for a reason.

His death could have occurred at any time, but it hadn't. The killer chose to strike when I was home for the first time in months.

Was that a sign?

Ambushed by Conscience

A lbert took a seat at the far end of the second row of chairs. They were arranged in a sort of semi-circle facing a pair of chairs at the front of the church hall. His plans for this evening had not included going to church, yet here he was, albeit in the hall attached to the side.

An emergency meeting of the church council had been called, by the vicar no less. Reverend David Gentry had been a fixture at the church for more than five years, working beneath the previous vicar Reverend Geoffrey Grey. However, Geoffrey had only retired a couple of months ago while Albert was on his tour of the British Isles.

Albert missed the whole thing, but Geoffrey was long overdue stepping down from the role and had only stayed on to help and guide his replacement. His brow creasing, Albert consulted his memory for facts about vicars and their tenures. He came up largely blank but thought it was unusual for there to be two men of the cloth ministering to the same parish for so many years.

Did that indicate something? He didn't know, so set the thought aside to be considered again another time.

Reverend David hadn't said why he wanted to get everyone together, but it wasn't a big leap to guess that it had to be because of Allen's murder.

Following Albert into his house, Roy had filled him in on what little he knew. Albert fed Rex, but with the clock ticking if he wanted to make it to the hastily arranged meeting, he settled for a ham and cheese sandwich – one of his personal specialities – and ate it on the way.

Rex was only too happy to be going out again. Snuggling up for a nap on the sofa with his human was a nice way to spend an evening, but not nearly so much fun as chasing criminals. He understood enough of what the humans around him said to know a murder had occurred.

The name, Allen Gibson - meant nothing to him, but it hardly mattered. A murder took place and the vicar asked for Albert by name.

While Rex was excited, the needle on Albert's own enthusiasm level failed to twitch. All he'd thought about for the last few weeks was leaving. His tour of the British Isles proved significantly more fraught with peril than expected and he'd been thoroughly glad to get home. However, media attention and constant recognition from the public everywhere he went made his already itchy feet yearn to escape once more.

He wasn't a member of the church council, and while he always attended when his wife, Petunia, insisted, it was far more her thing than his. Until only a few months before her passing, Petunia continued to be an active member of the community, most especially the church council.

Rex settled at the end of the pew, resting his head on his paws to wait until something interesting happened. He could smell tea brewing in the small kitchen set off to one side of the hall where the scent of digestive biscuits from a freshly opened packet called his name like a whispered promise.

Albert could hear the murmurs; other members of the church council questioning why he was there.

Looking around, he knew most of the people present. They were old faces from the village, people who had lived here for decades. Or since birth in many cases. There were a dozen of them, which meant a few were still to arrive.

The hall door swung wildly outward, the vicar bustling through it just a moment later. Close to forty, Reverend David was short and petite. He wore his blonde hair long and pulled into a rough ponytail that hung to his shoulder blades.

Albert didn't care for long hair on men, which is to say he would never let his grow that long and was glad neither of his sons had ever displayed an interest in longer styles. However, Albert would never comment and had to admit the long hair suited the vicar as it did many other men.

Rubbing his hands together to encourage warmth to circulate, the vicar greeted his assembled parishioners.

"Good evening, everyone. Thank you so much for coming at such short notice." He looked around. "I expect many of you know why I asked you to come this evening, but just in case that is not the ... um, case, it is my terrible duty to inform you that Allen Gibson has died."

There were several gasps. Albert expected that everyone knew, but that was clearly not the case.

Roy snuck into the chair next to Albert, leaning close to whisper, "I only know because I made him tell me why he wanted you. He called me because we are neighbours and begged that I bring you along."

"He wants me to solve the crime, doesn't he?"

"That would be my guess."

The vicar was moving through the attendees, offering sympathetic words. When he reached the front of the hall, he took one of the two seats facing all the others and waited for the church council to park themselves.

"Who sits in the other chair?" Albert asked Roy, his voice quiet so it would be heard only by his friend.

"The head of the church council, old boy. That used to be Angelica, but now it's the vicar's wife."

Albert knew Angelica Howard-Box and why she was no longer part of the church council. He'd had very few dealings with her which pleased him; she was rarely pleasant, and he'd never liked her; the woman was far too opinionated. However, he never imagined she would stoop to criminal enterprises to get her way. That she was now incarcerated and unlikely to return to the village during Albert's remaining years filled him with joy.

The vicar's wife was elsewhere it seemed, her seat empty.

"I'm sorry to have to burden you with even worse news," the vicar began, preparing the council for his next piece of news. "The truth of the matter is that Allen did not simply die, he was murdered."

This time the gasps were accompanied by a few shrieks of shock and a barrage of questions. The vicar weathered the storm, raising his hands to politely beg everyone to simmer down without needing to say the words.

"Needless to say the police are investigating, but this terrible and heinous crime occurred in the confines of our parish and that is why I have called you all here tonight." He let them think on that for a few seconds before continuing. "I believe the killer must have come from within our community."

His statement caused more gasps, these ones coming with a susurration of murmuring as the councillors began to argue among themselves.

The vicar had to raise his voice to be heard. "That is why I have asked Albert Smith to join us this evening."

Albert sat still when the conversation in the church hall ceased in an instant and every head turned his way. Roy gripped his shoulder in a supportive manner.

"Not just a retired senior detective with the Kent police, Albert, as I'm sure you all know, has a keen mind that recently exposed one of the biggest criminal scandals to grace the shores of our great nation."

Albert thought the vicar was laying it on more than a bit thick, but stayed quiet rather than argue. Ever since the Gastrothief story broke he'd been telling people he was lucky more than he was clever, but no one listened. Not even the king. They all thought he was being modest.

Turning his eyes to Albert, the vicar placed his hands together as if in prayer.

"Will you do this for us, Albert? Will you conduct your own investigation and help us to be sure the right person is brought to justice?"

Before he could answer, the hall door swung open again, a blast of cool air rushing in ahead of the person outside. Stumbling through the doorway and yanking it shut behind her was Mrs Gentry, the vicar's wife. Younger than her husband by most of a decade, she retained the vitality of youth and could easily pass for someone in their mid-twenties.

She was lean too, her figure the kind that most women would look at with envy. Showing that it was breezy outside, her hair was a mess, but she pulled it back into shape as she crossed the hall to join her husband.

"Hello everyone," she said with a touch more enthusiasm than the gathering called for. "Please excuse my tardiness. Where did we get to."

Sitting to Albert's left, Greta Hill grumbled, "Always got to make a big entrance." She made her remark at a volume that was lower than normal speech but most certainly loud enough that the vicar's wife would have heard it.

To Albert's mind the vicar looked displeased about his wife's late arrival. Naturally, he kept that emotion in check when he said, "I just asked Albert Smith to lead a private investigation into what happened to Allen."

The vicar's wife's face crinkled as she processed the news.

"Isn't he a bit old?" she asked.

Albert snorted a laugh; he couldn't help himself.

Cheeks flushing, the vicar's wife had nowhere to hide from her embarrassment.

"Oh, my goodness. I'm so sorry, I didn't mean that at all. What I meant was surely we should leave this to the police. There's no need to waste Mr Smith's time. The church doesn't have the funds to pay for his services anyway."

It was the vicar's turn to look embarrassed. "Oh, um, I hadn't thought about payment," he risked a glance at Albert.

"Of course you hadn't, dear," The vicar's wife rolled her eyes.

Albert ended the uncomfortable discussion. "I'm not in the habit of charging people." Honestly, it had never occurred to him. Albert solved a bunch of mysteries in his travels around England, and each time he did so because it was right in front of his face and someone was in trouble.

"There we go then," the vicar beamed.

Clearly still unhappy about it, his wife muttered, "That doesn't mean Mr Smith hasn't got better things to be doing with his time, David. The police are already on the case. Won't they take exception to his interference?"

"I'll be very discreet," interjected Albert, noting that he had somehow now volunteered to take the case even though it had never been his intention. It was like getting ambushed by his own conscience.

"He'll be very discreet," smiled the vicar, effectively settling the matter even though it was clear to everyone in the church hall that his wife was going to continue their conversation when they were in a less public setting.

Leaning close to whisper, Roy said, "He'll be in for it when he gets home."

With a thank you to everyone for coming, the vicar moved to the tea and coffee area, inviting his parishioners to stay for a while and remember Allen.

Albert thought about staying but knew he would be bombarded by endless questions were he to do so. Better to slip away and allow himself some time to gather his thoughts.

Nudging Roy with an elbow, he inclined his head toward the door.

"Pint?"

The Pub

T he old church, which was erected in Norman times, stood at the edge of the village. There were houses nearby, but none adjacent or opposite. Behind it, nothing but woodland stretched for miles until it met with the Tonbridge rail link.

Turning left outside the church hall, men and dog set off in a direction opposite to their homes.

There was a chill wind, but Rex didn't mind. His belly was full of dinner and the pub was in this direction. He could smell rabbits and the remains of something that hadn't moved fast enough to get out of the road. It was a couple of days old, his nose calculated, dismissing the scent as unimportant.

Albert could have gone straight home, he didn't need to go to the pub, but the quiet of his house drove him batty. It was one of the chief reasons why he was about to set off on another adventure though he told everyone a different story.

His entire married life had been in that house, and it still echoed with his wife's voice. Every now and then, even more than a year after her passing, he would walk into the kitchen and find himself surprised she wasn't there.

At the village pub, he held the door for his friend and then Rex to go inside where the warmth from a real fire filled the air with a scent that just cannot be faked. There was chatter and some background music, but no jukebox – it was very much not 'that' kind of establishment.

Over a couple of drinks, the men discussed what might have befallen poor Allen.

"I wonder what could have brought this about?" Roy voiced his thoughts. "I mean, I don't want to say anything bad about the poor chap, but he always came across as a bit boring. Too boring to get murdered I would have thought."

Albert drew in a deep breath through his nose. His years as a police detective exposed him to many murders. Some were premeditated, but most were 'heat of the moment' crimes the perpetrator wished they could take back. He could speculate about what befell the church treasurer, but doing so achieved nothing.

The man could have had a secret lover or even several. That alone could have resulted in his demise – affairs of the heart caused more unintended deaths than the public knew. Or it could have been money, the other favourite reason for someone getting killed. They were just two reasons though and he could name dozens more if he gave himself a few moments to compile a list.

Ultimately, whoever chose to stab the poor fellow probably felt justified in the moment. Their ire peaked at a level called murderous, but now they would feel guilt, shame, and fear at the possibility of getting caught. All too often it was the combination of emotions that gave a person away. They might be able to hide their awful truth in general, but when the police came calling few were cool enough to carry off the same lies they told their friends and family.

Rex enjoyed a packet of crisps and lapped at a bowl of water before settling in front of the fire to snooze. Above him the humans were chatting, discussing the murder case, but talking too quietly and too fast for Rex to make out enough of what they were saying.

He drifted off to sleep after a while, woken suddenly more than an hour later when Roy's phone rang.

Roy muttered an expletive under his breath.

"Beverly?" Albert guessed.

Roy pulled a face like he was sucking a lemon and picked up his phone. "Good evening, my queen."

"Don't you sweet talk me, Roy Hope."

Albert had no desire to eavesdrop, but Beverly's voice tended to carry.

"You told me the church council meeting was dragging on."

"It did drag on, my love."

"No, it didn't. I just got off the phone with Gwen Phelps and she said it lasted less than ten minutes."

Roy winced. "I might have exaggerated a tad."

Albert chuckled. He'd never knowingly misled his wife about anything, but Roy did it all the time and constantly got away with it. He just had one of those personalities that was permanently looking for the next bit of mischief.

"You're at the pub, aren't you?"

"Might be," Roy sighed. "I shall drink up and be home soon."

"Oh, no you won't. You'll order me a double gin and tonic and be ready for me with a bag of scampi fries. I'm already putting on my coat."

The line went dead, and Roy hung his head.

"Busted," he muttered. "Again."

Chuckling still, Albert picked up his glass to drain the final inch of liquid.

"That's enough for me."

"You're leaving, old boy?" Roy looked horrified at the notion. "Abandoning a chap in the face of the enemy?"

Albert collected his coat and stood. "She's your wife, Roy, and you are jolly lucky to have her."

Trapped by the unintended consequences of his actions, Roy stayed behind to wait for his wife, but promised to look Albert up the next day to assist in his investigation.

Outside in the cold air, Albert thought to hurry straight home, but it wasn't much of a detour to swing by Allen's house. Nearing it, Albert slowed. The property was dark, and though crime scene tape remained in place on the front door and around the garden gate, the officers tasked with investigating the case were long gone.

He could get into the house if he so chose, but that was against the law and would contaminate a scene the police might wish to reexamine.

Rex pulled at his lead, sniffing the air.

"*Is this the place?*" he asked. "*It smells of lots of people. Dozens of them.*" A scent caught in his nose, a familiar one that he hadn't detected in a long while. It was a person from the village, a friendly person he would know if he saw her again.

Albert tugged Rex back. "We're not going in, boy."

"*But I need to smell where the killer was,*" Rex explained. "*Come on, old man, you know how this works well enough.*" He needed to be able to smell the clues, plus, if he understood correctly, the murder was only a day old, so he stood a chance of finding the killer's scent among the odours in the house.

Another gentle tug on his lead got Rex moving, Albert keeping him close to his side. He was about to cross the road when movement caught the corner of his eye.

There was someone in the house!

Sic 'im, Rex!

The lights were off, the person inside using a small torch to see their way. Whoever it was had no business being there, that went without saying, but what possible reason could they have for snooping in a dead man's house after dark? That he was witness to the killer returning to the scene of the crime resounded in Albert's head.

His heart doubled its pace; not out of fear, but because he knew what he was going to do next.

Folding at the waist to get closer to Rex's ears – much easier than bending his knees and trying to get back up afterward – he whispered, "Rex, I think it might be time to chase a killer. Are you up for it?"

Rex almost barked with excitement and only just managed to control it. Muscles tense, he wanted his human to unclip his lead, but the wind wasn't giving him a scent to know which direction to go.

"*Where?*" Rex asked, his voice quiet.

Albert had no idea his dog was asking a question, and was already going through the gate to get to Allen's front door. The killer was inside, and if it wasn't the killer, they still needed to explain themselves to the police.

Justifying his decision to break into the house by telling himself he could close the case and save the police wasted manhours and thus the taxpayers a pile of money, he readied a rock. Putting it through the small window next to the door would allow him to reach through to operate the lock. The sound would alert the intruder instantly, but Rex was fast enough that it wouldn't matter.

Raising the rock, he was just about to strike when a stray thought made him check the handle. It turned, the door opening inward. With his other hand gripping Rex's collar – the only way to be sure he could keep hold of him – Albert threw the rock back onto the garden and unclipped the dog's lead.

Rex needed no further encouragement, but the simple command of, "Rex, sic 'im!" put an extra burst of energy in his initial leap.

The house was unfamiliar; he'd never been in it before, and it was filled with conflicting scents from dozens of people. Expecting to have a dominant smell to chase, he had to pause and use his ears before setting off.

That was all the time the other person in the house needed to realise it was time to go. They heard a voice and a bark and knew precisely what they both meant.

Rex barrelled through the house, turning left and right as he tried to pinpoint where he needed to go. Hearing, like eyesight, is far from reliable, so when he finally caught a fresh scent he surged forward with confidence, following it to the source.

Also hurrying through the house, Albert was yet to hear his dog snarl or a person cry out in fear or pain when a door slammed shut.

Was it the back door he heard? He thought so and made a beeline for the kitchen.

Rex barked, voicing his frustration though Albert could barely tell the difference from one bark to the next.

Albert found his dog at the back door, twitching with excitement and unable to get out.

"*He went that way!*" Rex barked. "*Let me out! I can still catch him!*"

26

Albert snatched the door open, yanking it inward against the pressure of Rex impatiently attempting to exit.

The dog burst free, shooting into the darkness behind the house just as a car's interior lights came on beyond the hedge at the garden's boundary.

For a fleeting moment, the figure clambering inside found themselves framed in the light. They flicked the switch to kill it, but by then it was too late: Albert had seen who it was.

Rex reached the end of the garden where he had to slow and use a paw to hook the gate open. The car's engine burst to life, leaving Rex behind in a plume of exhaust gasses when the driver floored his pedal.

Rex also knew who the driver was; he'd gotten a good whiff of his scent in the house and again following him from it. Not only was it one he recognised, he'd been given a refresher just a couple of hours ago.

With his head down, he charged after the car, but he knew from experience that he wasn't going to be able to catch it. In theory he could track the car so long as it didn't go too far, but concern for his human made him stop after a hundred yards.

Backtracking to the house, Rex found the old man standing in the street. Albert had chosen to pause at the back door before following his dog, but only long enough to check the key inserted into the lock. A few feet to the right, an obvious rock was out of place where Albert guessed the key normally hid. It explained how the intruder got in, but not what he was there for.

Albert ruffled Rex's fur and patted his head. With the dog lead reattached, he started toward their home.

To say he felt troubled would be an understatement. He wanted time to think before acting, that was the crux of it. Had it been anyone else's face illuminated by the car's interior light, Albert would have already called the police.

However, the sight of the vicar fleeing the house of a murdered man only hours after requesting, in person, that Albert catch the killer, begged some investigation.

Silent Witness

- -

"**P**atty! It's time for fitness!" boomed Barbie, throwing my curtains open with gusto and vigour.

She was already dressed in spandex that made her bottom look like two perfectly rounded pillows. I could wear the same exact garment and my bum would also look like a pillow.

After someone had been sitting on it for many hours.

I gripped my duvet. "I can't," I tried. "I have a cold. Aaaaachoooo!"

Barbie giggled.

"Seriously, Barbie. It's too early, I don't feel well, my feet ache."

She put her hands on her hips and narrowed her eyes at me.

"Remember when you told me I shouldn't listen to any of your excuses because you're in the best shape of your life and you genuinely love feeling strong and flexible."

Me and my stupid mouth.

"Yes, but I have a note this time."

"A note?" Barbie's perfect left eyebrow set itself at a questioning angle. "From whom?"

"Um, from me."

Barbie shook her head and started toward the door, grabbing my sports clothes and throwing them on my bed as she left.

"Five minutes, lazybones or I'll make it a double session."

An hour later, skin pink from the shower, legs and bottom feeling like they'd been attacked by a meat tenderiser from all the squats and lunges, I settled into a chair for breakfast.

The truth is that I do prefer the fitter version of me. I just don't like the effort it takes to maintain it. Going to the gym with Barbie fills me with dread to the point that I struggle to sleep some nights. You might think I could convince her to go a little easier; I'm well into my fifties after all, but whenever I try that I somehow find myself doing an additional fifty pushups or something.

Sashaying in to join me and showing no sign that she had matched me in the gym by doing two reps to every one of mine, Barbie waved to Jermaine and took the seat opposite me.

"Where's Hideki?" I asked.

"Just coming. He had a lie in."

I gritted my teeth and kept my words inside.

"Have you decided what to do?" she asked.

She lost me for a second until I realised she must mean Allen Gibson.

I nodded. "Yes, I'm going to ask a few questions."

Barbie's eyes sparkled; my answer pleased her.

Jermaine, who asked after my breakfast preferences earlier, plated up for both Barbie and me and brought our food to the table.

Scrambled eggs with smashed, spiced avocado, grilled bacon, and wholewheat toast. A feast really, but one I had earned. Moreover, Barbie, my nutritionist as well as my fitness instructor, approved.

Tucking in, I arranged my thoughts.

"I will start at the post office."

"With Mavis?" Barbie checked.

"Are you joining us, sweetie?" I asked Jermaine. Yes, he's my butler, but only because he insists he needs to be. I would be quite happy to have him do next to nothing other than protect me from harm.

"Just as soon as Hideki arrives, madam."

Mercifully, Barbie's boyfriend wandered in the very next moment and once the four of us were settled, I continued with what I was saying.

"Mavis mentioned hearing a woman was seen leaving Allen's house late the night he was killed. I wasn't really paying attention at the time and cannot recall the identity of the witness."

"Are you going to call Sam?" Barbie asked me about my assistant.

I thought about it for a second, but shook my head. "No, I think he will benefit from a break. We'll all be back together soon enough."

Breakfast finished, there was no reason to delay getting on with our day. I took a little time to make myself presentable, but a touch of hair and makeup was all it needed.

Hideki stayed behind when the rest of us set off in my Range Rover. Still in his first year as a qualified doctor he had all sorts of study to complete, and these few days off were the ideal opportunity to catch up.

Jermaine steered us through the village. It was walking distance, in truth, but with no way to tell where we might need to go next, it was prudent to have the car at our disposal.

The village was quiet. Admittedly, it usually is, but today it seemed more so as though the murder had somehow caused everyone to stay indoors. Driving through the village we didn't pass a single car save for those parked outside houses and when we arrived at the post office the small carpark was empty.

Inside we found Sharon looking bored at the cash register. She glanced up from a magazine, performing a double take when she saw who it was.

I was through the door and already moving away from her though, heading to the back and the post office counter where I expected to find Mavis.

She saw me coming.

"Caught the killer yet?" she cackled. She had a stack of mail piled high in front of her on the counter, but it got shoved to one side so she could talk to me.

"Not yet," I replied. "It's why I am here, actually."

"Didn't think it was a social call."

Mavis wasn't one for small talk unless it was juicy gossip. Then she could talk all day.

"Mavis, you said yesterday that someone saw a woman leaving the house the night Allen was killed. Remind me who that someone was, please."

"It was old Mrs Forrester," Mavis offered up the answer before I could finish asking my question.

"Beryl Forrester?" I confirmed.

Mavis was already moving to the end of the counter, pulling off the apron she always wears for work. Shouting to make sure Sharon heard her, she said, "I'm popping out. If anyone moans about the post office being shut," she paused to turn the open sign around so it showed the word 'closed' instead, "tell 'em to get stuffed. I'm helping Patricia Fisher solve a murder."

This wasn't exactly what I had in mind. Clearly Mavis was coming with us to Mrs Forrester's house, but it wasn't as if I could order her to get back to work.

Dumping her apron, she vanished from sight for two seconds through a door at the end of the counter, reappearing when another door opened into the shop.

"Beryl has a shot of whisky in her coffee at this time of the day," Mavis continued to show how much she knew about everyone in the village. "She says it gets her blood pumping. If we don't dally we might get there in time to join her."

Barbie showed me wide eyes, the idea of whisky at this time of the day clearly a little alien to her. Personally, it didn't appeal, but I could understand the sentiment. Getting old isn't easy, so if a belt of something strong is what makes a person feel ready to tackle their day, good for them. Plus, when you reach a certain age, you care little for the opinions of others and don't worry too much about the negative effects of the foods and other vices you might have steered clear of at a younger age.

"It's walking distance," I told Jermaine and Barbie, so they would know we didn't need to take the car.

Mavis was all set to take the shortcut through the trees, but one look at our shoes, built for style or, in Barbie's case, running really fast, and she changed her mind.

"We'll take the long route," she announced, setting off along the pavement.

Even the long route, as she called it, wasn't exactly far and we arrived at Beryl Forrester's door six minutes later.

Waiting for her to answer, I dredged my memory to recall when I last spoke with one of the village's oldest residents. It would probably have been a year ago or more and almost certainly at church. I could half remember a conversation about her tom cat getting fat only to then produce a litter of six kittens. One of them was in the window now, staring at us with all the benevolent disinterest a cat can muster.

"No answer," said Mavis, pressing the doorbell for what had to be the fourth or fifth time. Abruptly, she bent at the waist, stuck her fingers into the letterbox to hold it open and shouted, "Beryl, it's Mavis! Are you there?"

Barbie pressed her face up against the glass of a window looking into the living room. With her hands around her eyes to shield the glare, she declared there to be no sign of life.

I didn't like her choice of phrase.

Jermaine cut his eyes at me. "Perhaps I should check around the back, madam," he suggested, his tone cautiously not expressing the worry now beginning to rise.

"Please do, sweetie," I encouraged.

To the left of the house, a double-fronted bungalow, a six-foot-high wooden gate led to the back garden. It was locked on the other side with a sliding bolt. However, with his height, all Jermaine needed to do was reach his arm over and feel around to find it.

I chose to go with him, hoping I might lessen the shock when Beryl looked up to see a large black man outside her kitchen window.

However, there was no sign of her in the back rooms of the house either.

"Could she have gone out?" asked Barbie as she and Mavis came to join us.

Mavis drawled, "Nah. Old Mrs Forrester doesn't go anywhere, love. She's ninety-nine. A trip to the post office once or twice a week because through the trees it's not all that far and she's surprisingly sprightly once she's had her morning nip of the good stuff. Plus, she goes to the pub on a Thursday because it's quiz night and she's old enough to know everything. She gets a lift there though on account of it being a bit far to walk home once she's had a few."

I felt rather than saw Jermaine stiffen.

He said, "Madam," in a meaningful way and was shoulder barging the back door open by the time I turned around to look his way.

That we were about to find Mrs Forrester on the floor was a grim certainty, but even coming through the back door I expected the old dear to be alive.

Barbie held onto the kitchen counter, drawing a slow, calming breath. No one said anything, not even Mavis who normally won't shut up unless you are spilling secrets for her to share with the rest of the village.

Beryl Forrester wouldn't get her letter from the king upon her next birthday. That she was no longer with us was completely obvious. So much so that no one bothered to check her pulse.

There was olive oil on the floor and a pool of it where the bottle had come to rest a few feet away. One leg was bent behind her body, making it look like she was trying to perform the splits. Her arms were out to her sides, the left partially hidden beneath a thin chopping board. On her right she wore a wristwatch, the face of which was smashed to obscure the time.

If one took the scene at face value, Beryl had been making dinner. There was a saucepan on the stove containing two small potatoes, a portion of sliced beef in gravy ready made to be heated in the oven, and scattered around her the peelings and slices of a carrot clearly intended for a second, smaller pot still sitting on the counter where the chopping board must once have been.

She had spilled the oil and slipped in it, breaking her neck as she hit the ground. That was what it looked like anyway.

Mavis was the first to speak.

"I'd better get back to the post office," she murmured, her eyes still locked on Beryl's body. She didn't say that she had new juicy gossip to share and I chose not to accuse her, there being no need for a face-to-face confrontation, but I believed that to be the reason for her hasty departure.

"We'll call the police," I let her know as she backed toward the door.

"Yes, of course ..." she mumbled. "Sure, right. You call the police."

Jermaine opened the kitchen door to let her out and stepped outside himself to not be in the way. Meanwhile, I looked at Barbie.

Her expression was grim, as it ought to be standing in the presence of a dead person.

"Murdered?" she asked.

I shrugged a shoulder. "Hard to say. She could have simply slipped."

Barbie sagged a little. "Come on, Patty, this is you we're talking about."

I raised both eyebrows.

"It's always murder, Patty. Everywhere you go someone is getting offed. I'm not suggesting that you are in any way the catalyst ... more like God has a purpose for each of us and yours is to solve heinous crimes so he makes sure you show up just when one is happening."

I dearly wanted to argue, but she kinda had a point and I rather liked the idea that a higher power was behind my constant influx of crimes to investigate.

One thing was for sure, we had to call the police and vacate the building while we waited for their arrival.

I started in the direction of the back door, but stopped after only a step and backtracked, picking where to place my feet so I wouldn't disturb anything.

"Whatcha doing, Patty?" Barbie enquired.

"Her watch is broken," I replied. "I noticed it when we first walked in. Don't you think that's a little unusual?"

Barbie shrugged. "I guess it broke in the fall. She must have landed pretty hard."

I didn't touch Beryl's watch or her arm, and used my knuckles to support my weight so I wouldn't leave fingerprints on the kitchen floor when I leaned right down to see the watch.

"Just after half past eight," I noted. Beryl had the body of a soup chicken. She couldn't weigh more than ninety pounds. Would she have landed heavily enough to smash the face of her watch? There was no obvious way to test that theory and it was possible she broke it days, weeks, or even months ago.

However, assuming it broke when she hit the ground, the watch told us what time she died.

I clambered back to my feet, again without touching anything, and said a prayer as I moved away. There was no sign of a struggle and the doors at the front and back of the house were both locked from the inside until Jermaine forced his way inside.

Was Barbie right? Had Beryl met with a terrible accident or was her death the result of seeing the killer leaving Allen Gibson's house on the opposite side of the street?

Outside in Beryl's back garden, not looking its best at this time of the year, I made the call, gave them the address, and hoped they wouldn't be too long. Little did I know a friend of mine was already on his way to explore a lead for the first murder.

Unexpected Arrest

Albert watched the path ahead for squirrels. They were plentiful in the area and seemed to view antagonising his dog as some kind of sport. Each time one of them darted out from a tree or ran across the road thirty yards ahead, Rex would twitch. Albert supposed he couldn't help himself.

Padding along the pavement at the extent of his leather lead, Rex scanned the horizon. One of the squirrels was going to mess up and get too close. When that happened, he was going to be ready. Getting to it would mean yanking the lead from his human's hand, for which he already felt bad, though to his mind it was necessary.

He would chase and catch the fluffy menace which would squeal and complain and learn a valuable lesson to take home to the rest of its friends and family. And home to its family Rex would let it go, once he'd carried it around in his mouth for an hour or two, whispering all the things he could do to it with just the slightest tense of his jaw muscles.

Oh, the fluffy menace would rue the day. Rue it!

Unable to hear the thoughts in his dog's head, Albert's own thoughts, when not focused on scanning the way ahead, above, and behind for members of the squirrel mafia, were firmly locked on the parish vicar.

There was no mistake, no stray thought that his eyes might have deceived him. He knew what he had seen, and it was Reverend David diving into his car to make a quick getaway. The vicar had been inside the home of the recently murdered church treasurer looking for something with a torch.

That he chose to not turn on the lights made it clear he didn't wish to have his snooping discovered. Furthermore, the vicar parked his car at the back of the house by the garages, not out the front under the streetlights where it might have been seen.

The question of what he might have been looking for kept Albert awake past midnight. It was most troubling. On one hand, Albert knew with absolute certainty that the vicar had to have a perfectly good and justifiable explanation for his late night breaking and entering. At the same time, Albert knew members of the clergy could be just as underhanded and criminal as anyone else and had witnessed it first hand himself many years ago.

It left him facing a conundrum, but one which had a simple solution. Since he saw the vicar, chances were that Reverend David knew who chased him from the house. Assuming that to be the case, Albert was on his way to ask the vicar a few very pointed questions.

He hoped it would be something simple such as the vicar knowing Allen possessed a collection of dirty magazines or videos he wouldn't want the world to know about. The vicar could have been taking them to be destroyed. Truthfully, Albert doubted it would be anything so benign. At any rate, as he turned the penultimate corner before reaching Vicarage Lane, he believed he would find out the truth soon enough.

However, the familiar crackle of a radio brought his attention back to the here and now. It put extra haste into his step too. Rounding the final corner, his worst fears were confirmed: there were cops outside the vicarage.

Sucking air through his teeth, Albert stopped at the corner to observe. No less than three squad cars were parked in the street with two officers in uniform visible. They were eighty yards away, directly in front of the driveway leading into the vicarage.

Albert had been inside once ... no, twice, he corrected himself. Both times at Petunia's insistence. As an active member of the church council, she got invited to Christmas drinks and nibbles and other such events. He generally managed to dodge attending, but a man can only take so much pressure from his wife before knowing to cave is the wiser option.

Debating his new options, Albert clicked his tongue and started walking.

Rex could smell the vicar and now understood the reason for the route they took. Morning walks were almost always the same, and he could not recall ever coming this way before. However, he recognised there had been a murder – the humans said so, and running through the dead man's house the previous evening he'd been able to smell the abundance of blood even though a clean-up crew had removed the worst of it.

He chased a man he knew, a man who had stood at the front of the room talking before they left that place to go to the pub the previous evening. That the same man was in the dead man's house confused Rex, but his human gave the order to chase, so Rex had done just that.

The man got away, which was always disappointing, but Rex's wily old human was once again proving how clever humans could be by leading him to where the target lived.

Was he the killer? Rex hadn't worked that part out yet and was glad to have the old man as a sidekick for he was good at the things Rex struggled to do. Regardless, his nose picked out the fresh scent of the man which meant he was now outside of his house.

Albert saw the vicar a second after Rex caught his scent. He was being led to a waiting police squad car in cuffs. It made Albert's eyes almost pop from his head.

The sight was followed instantly by the sound of the vicar's wife wailing.

"Why, David? Why? Why would you do this to us?"

The vicar struggled against the police officer holding his arm. A second officer had gone ahead, holding the door open and probably expecting zero resistance from the man of God.

Twisting around to make eye contact with his wife, Reverend David Gentry said, "But I'm innocent darling! You must know that! I could never kill a man."

Mrs Gentry appeared in the street, emerging from behind the thick hedge bordering the vicarage. Now able to see the entire scene, Albert felt like an intruder, a peeping Tom almost. He was witness to a domestic discussion he had no right to view.

Mrs Gentry had tears streaming down her face, tracks of mascara running over her cheeks she made no attempt to remove.

"But they have the evidence, David!" she screamed in his face.

A little bewildered by the turn of events, the cops were slow to react. They needed to get the suspect into the squad car and Mrs Gentry back inside her house. There would be questions to ask, and they might choose to take her to the station later. For now, Albert knew, they would tread as gently as they could, teasing information rather than forcing it.

The officer holding the car door open moved to grip the vicar's other arm. Between them the two cops began to wrestle the still protesting vicar to the squad car.

They employed polite words of encouragement. "Come along now, Sir. This isn't helping anyone." And "Now, now, vicar."

It was almost amusing to Albert who knew the language for any other suspect would be starkly different.

"But I'm innocent!" the vicar insisted, his voice raised and forceful. His body angled away from the car, his feet digging in to impede the officers now manhandling him.

"Oh, David," wailed his wife once more. "What did you even need the money for?"

Money? There was money involved? Albert heard the question, and it shocked him. Sure, they were talking about the murder of the church treasurer, but how much money did he handle on a weekly basis? A few hundred? Less? They took a collection at the Sunday service, but other than that what other forms of income were there?

The questions were still rattling around in his head when a familiar voice said, "Quite so?"

The voice was followed by the equally familiar, yet very much unwelcome face of Chief Inspector Quinn. He stepped out from behind the hedge, sidestepped Mrs Gentry to crowd the vicar.

"You will tell me everything very soon, Reverend, and that which you choose to hide will be uncovered by my detectives." His words, his calm superior air and certainty took the fight out of the vicar. When he slumped, Quinn sneered at the constables holding his arms, "Now stop embarrassing yourselves and take him away."

Albert watched, his jaw set and his mind whirring from a distance of twenty feet. The vicar was accused of the treasurer's murder, and it had something to do with money. If these things were true, it went some way to explain his presence in Allen Gibson's house the previous evening.

The chief inspector turned away when the door to the squad car slammed shut with the vicar inside. In so doing he caught sight of the old man and his dog. Both were watching him with the same intense gaze.

Albert waited for the loathsome senior officer to say something, but all he got was a tight narrowing of Quinn's eyes.

Using an arm to shepherd Mrs Gentry, Quinn ushered her back toward the house leaving Albert and Rex in the street.

Rex looked up at his human. "*Now what?*"

His lips skewed to one side, Albert was asking himself much the same question. All night he fretted over his discovery and what to do about it. Many would argue he ought to have called the police straight away. He hadn't though, convinced there had to be a rational, non-murderous explanation for the vicar's breaking and entering.

Now it seemed that there was not. Yet the vicar asked for Albert by name. He contacted Roy with a plea to bring Albert to an emergency meeting at the church hall where he then begged him to find Allen Gibson's killer.

Why do any of that if he was the killer? To throw doubt? Albert didn't believe that for a second. It was the oldest trick in the book and never worked.

Adding up the few meagre facts he possessed told Albert nothing, they just encouraged confusion. Ruminating on the subject, Albert started walking again. He was halfway home when a speeding squad car shot past him.

It was moving fast but without sirens or lights which either meant the cops inside were late for a meal or needed to be somewhere in a hurry. He was on the main artery through East Malling, if the narrow lane could be called that, and got to see when the car turned right into Barnes Street.

Whatever they were racing to get to was in the village. Curious, and already walking in that direction, Albert crossed the road.

Old Friends

"**M**rs Fisher?" asked the police officer, a young man I did not recognise. He was just donning his hat, the car door still open. On the other side, the driver, a female officer, was also getting out.

With the police on their way, Barbie, Jermaine, and I chose to move back to the front of the house where they would see us.

"Yes," I identified myself though I doubted he needed me to given that my face had been splashed across the world's newspapers ever since the San José story broke three days ago.

Both cops joined us in front of Beryl's house. They looked to be in their mid-twenties. The man had thick black hair and tan skin, his partner red hair and skin so white it made me question when she had last seen the sun.

"I'm Constable Rankin," the female introduced herself. "This is Constable Rowe."

"She's this way," I announced, inclining my head.

Jermaine held the gate open, and I led the cops around the back of Beryl's house to the kitchen door where they could see for themselves.

"You forced the door?" Rankin asked. It was a confirmation, not an accusation. Anyone would have forced the door when they saw the little old lady's legs sticking out from behind her kitchen table.

"That was me," said Jermaine.

Rankin and Rowe donned gloves before touching the door and were careful not to use the handle when they levered it open.

We left them to it, remaining outside though I was beginning to get cold, and the warmth of Beryl's house proved enticing.

"Should I fetch the car, madam?" asked Jermaine, proving I was doing a poor job of hiding how I felt.

"Yes, please, dear."

Barbie seconded the motion.

However, Jermaine returned less than ten seconds after going out through the back garden's side gate. I was about to question if he'd forgotten something or if I had the key when a nose came through the gate behind him.

It belonged to a large German Shepherd dog. One of the largest I have ever seen, in fact. Half a second later, the owner appeared, his right hand looped through a lead attached to the dog's collar.

"Albert!" I cried with genuine happiness. I hadn't seen Albert Smith in many months and had gasped with surprise when I saw his name in the paper the first time. The last time we spoke, I could recall it vividly, was right around when my cook, Pamela Ellis, went on a murderous rampage over a baking competition.

I had bumped into Albert outside the post office and learned of his intention to take a culinary tour of the British Isles. It ought to have been a pleasant trip around our fair shores, yet I knew from the news articles that he encountered murder and mayhem almost everywhere he went. That it ended in a secret bunker beneath a Welsh hill with a member of the royal family holding a mass of chefs captive was beyond belief, yet true, nonetheless.

"Wait," said Barbie, not that I did. I was surging forward to give my old friend a hug. "Is that Albert Smith?" she asked.

"Albert," I repeated, putting my arms around him in an embrace that was far more familiar than we were used to. So much in my life had changed since I caught my husband in bed with another woman at the start of the summer and clearly Albert had endured something similar. Fame was thrust upon us, his face vying for the front page as often as mine in recent months. "And Rex," I let go of Albert to lavish his gorgeous dog with equal attention.

Rex wagged his tail at me and leaned in to deepen my fur ruffling activities.

"This is Beryl Forrester's house?" Albert asked a rhetorical question. "Is she?"

I nodded. "Do you know about Allen Gibson?"

It was Albert's turn to nod, but I could see from the set of his eyebrows there was more.

"I ...um, I was asked to investigate who killed him by the vicar last night. He called the church council to an emergency meeting."

"Oh." That was news to me. "Well, that's good. I guess. I was thinking about looking into the case myself. That's what led me here. Mrs Forrester told Mavis she saw someone leaving Allen's house last night."

We both angled our eyes in the direction of Allen's house. It wasn't visible from our current location due to the fence, but sat on the opposite side of the road. Beryl would have a good view of his property from either of the rooms at the front of her house.

Albert wriggled his lips around in thought before saying, "The vicar was just arrested for his murder."

I almost spat out my teeth. "What?"

Barbie echoed my thoughts, but said, "You've got to be kidding."

"I wish I were," replied Albert, his voice solemn. "I'm afraid there's more."

He came a step closer, checking over the top of my head to see Rowe and Rankin inside. I believed he was checking they couldn't hear us, an assumption confirmed a few moments later when he dropped his voice to a whisper.

"Walking home from the pub last night I came past Allen's house. There was someone inside."

The way he said it I knew who he was going to claim to have seen before he told me. "It was the vicar, wasn't it."

"Don't be daft, Patty," Barbie gasped.

Albert flicked his eyes to her and then back to me. "I'm afraid it was the vicar. He fled when I set Rex loose, but I caught sight of him when he got into his car. It was the vicar, of that there is no doubt."

Focussing on the facts, rather than the disbelief rampaging through my brain, I asked, "What else do you know?"

Albert huffed out a breath, unhappy to know all that he did.

"It all has something to do with money. His wife was shouting at him when they led him away. If we take the clues at face value, the vicar murdered the church treasurer over money. I had a quick look around Allen's after the vicar got away. I saw which room he was searching, but he either found it and took what he was after with him, or the police already found it. Whatever the vicar wanted so badly he chose to break in to find it remains a secret for now."

It was damning for sure, but did I really believe the vicar could be Allen's killer? If so it stood to reason he killed Beryl too and the man I thought I knew wouldn't do either thing.

The sound of approaching sirens ended our conversation. Constable Rowe heard them too, leaving the house via the backdoor.

"Sorry, folks, I need you to vacate the premises."

"Yes, of course," I replied. "This is now a crime scene."

Rowe was heading for the gate to get back to the street, but stopped and turned to face me, his face set with a quizzical expression.

"Crime scene? Why ever would you think that?"

I jinked an eyebrow, but Barbie spoke first. "Because the little old lady was murdered."

Rowe shook his head as if to clear it. "She slipped on an oil spill while making her dinner. I would have thought that was obvious. Not every death is murder," he replied as though we were all being ridiculous. Moving to open the gate, he held it that way. "Now, if you please."

The request was nothing of the sort. The cops had a dead body to deal with and even though they believed Beryl's death to be accidental, there was no good reason for any of us to be hanging around.

We could be in the street – that's a public right of way - but they would likely cordon off a chunk of it if people began to gather.

Regardless, all such thoughts exited stage left when the next police car pulled to sharp stop behind the first. I was just coming onto the pavement and had prime view of the face glaring at me from the passenger seat.

"Oh, goody," I sighed. "Chief Inspector Quinn."

Old Enemies

"**B**oth of you?" he growled, exiting his car with a face a normal man could only achieve if they were to find their car had been clamped and the bill for releasing came attached to an arrow through the neck fired by their ex-wife that then turned out to be on fire.

"Good morning, Chief Inspector," I replied brightly, a warm smile displayed to match my words.

Albert chuckled instead. "Better either of us than one of you, dummy. How is it that you get to keep wearing that uniform when you disgrace it just by putting it on?"

Riled, Quinn closed the distance, aiming to get into Albert's face but forgetting the dog.

Rex reared on his hind legs, barking at the chief inspector and only held in check by his human.

"Get him under control, old man, or I shall call animal control," sneered Quinn.

Stepping around me, Barbie held up her camera. "Smile, dummy, you're being recorded." Her big grin spread to the rest of us.

"Any more threats?" I enquired. "Any more unprovoked, unpleasant remarks you wish to aim our way?"

I got seething silence in return.

"There is no need for us to be enemies, Chief Inspector," I soothed.

"Speak for yourself," said Albert. "The idiot organised a nationwide manhunt for me. I was on the run for weeks because I tried to help."

"You were wanted for questioning and refused to come forward," Quinn snapped. "Solving crimes and catching criminals is my job, not yours."

"And yet you are so bad at it we have to keep getting involved," Albert shot back without needing to consider his response.

Trying, yet again, to instil some calm, I said, "Look, Ian, we are not here to cause any delay to your investigation ..."

"And yet I find myself unable to reach my destination because you bar my way."

I stepped aside, Jermaine helpfully reaching back to open Beryl's garden gate.

Instantly, he dismissed us all, forging through the gap to get away. Before he could get out of earshot, I said, "Mrs Forrester saw someone coming out of Allen's Gibson's house late on the night that he was killed."

The chief inspector stopped, one hand on the gate. Without turning around he asked, "Who?"

I was glad he asked that particular question the way he did because it lent well to the answer I wanted to give.

"She was killed before we could find that out. However, she reported that it was a woman."

Rotating on his heels to look back at our group, he said, "Killed? You think this to be another murder?" He wasn't here because an old lady slipped, fell, and died in her house. Whatever else I might say or think about him, he recognised the terrible coincidence in two deaths a day apart in the same street.

"I do. You will find the scene well set, it looks like she slipped and fell, but the likelihood she was deliberately silenced is too great."

The chief inspector appeared to consider my statement for a moment, and I thought he was going to ask me a question. However, he turned about again without another word and was lost to sight around the side of the house a moment later.

Albert muttered a word to describe him.

Barbie nodded. "He really is. A big one at that."

The constable who arrived with Quinn hurried after his boss when the chief inspector barked his name. It left the four of us in the street. Five, I suppose, if one chooses to include Rex.

"Join forces?" Albert suggested.

I never really wanted to investigate what happened to Allen Gibson and only set out to ask Mrs Forrester a couple of questions to learn if she had seen anything of worth. However, with the vicar in custody, the suggestion that money could be at the core of the mystery, and with Quinn all but throwing down the gauntlet, was there really a choice?

Tea and Plans

- -

At my house, Jermaine provided refreshment in the form of tea and sandwiches. We were gathered around the kitchen table – the casual hub of the house – rather than one of the formal dining spaces or reception rooms. I prefer the kitchen simply because it is more comfortable. The Maharaja gifted me this enormous house, and I love it, but it's a bit too big for me. A person needs to have ten children plus their children living in it for it to begin to feel filled with life.

Having determined that both Albert and I were going to investigate the murders, we needed to discuss how to divide up the tasks and coordinate.

"I would like to get into both properties," Albert announced. "There will be physical clues if one knows what to look for."

"What sort of thing?" asked Jermaine, delivering a second silver tray of tea with all the trimmings.

Albert already had a sandwich in one hand and a plate in the other to catch the crumbs. Swallowing his mouthful, he said, "Method of entry for one. You said neither the back door nor the front appeared to have been forced at Beryl's house. That plays well into the theory that Mrs Forrester fell and her death was accidental. However, if we operate under the assumption she was murdered, the killer had to gain entry."

"So either they were known to Mrs Forrester, and she let them in ..." said Barbie.

"Or they had a key," I finished.

Albert nodded. "Or they knew where to find the spare key. When I chased the vicar from Allen's house last night, there was a rock overturned where Allen kept his spare key hidden. The vicar might have turned over plants pots and rocks until he found it, but chances are he knew where to find it. It could be the same for Mrs Forrester's house."

"Yes," I agreed, "but I don't think the vicar did it."

"Why not?" asked Albert, adding, "I mean, I want to believe you are right and I hope we can prove it, but you sound certain and I'm curious as to why."

What did I say to explain my odd 'sixth' sense?

"Her skull itches when she senses the truth," blurted Barbie.

Albert tilted his head quizzically, his expression begging that I explain.

Feeling heat in my cheeks, I said, "Thank you, Barbie." I got a grin from her in response, and I knew what she was doing – getting her own back for all the times I refuse to tell her what I have figured out. "She's right, in a way. I have a strange ability to know when I have finally figured out the answer."

Albert accepted my answer and moved on. "Anyway, it won't be easy to get back inside those houses. With the second murder the cops will be all over them today. Instead, I think I will look at the vicar, unless that's what you were planning."

He was deferring to me and being gracious, offering me the pick of investigative routes.

"No, please," I replied. "We only know the vicar was searching for something in Allen's house because you caught him. You're also the one who learned the case might be to do with money."

"Then I shall take Rex and do some digging."

"Damn skippy," barked Rex. *"I need to get back to the crime scenes though. I know we won't get inside, but I'll be able to get a half decent scent sample from the doors. The trace of each person to touch them won't linger long, but that's kind of the point – only the most recent scents will remain."*

Giving Rex a pat and an ear scratch since he was right next to me, I focused my thoughts on what I would do. Whoever killed Allen did so for a reason. Taking that as separate from the vicar's need to raid Allen's house looking for something yet to be identified, I wanted to know who Allen had been seen with recently.

Did he have a woman in his life? Or a man? I believed he was straight, but who really knows what secrets a person keeps. Where did he go? What habits did he keep? These questions were little more than starting points, but each would lead me somewhere or nowhere and both things could be useful.

I also questioned the value in visiting the vicar himself. He'd only just been arrested, so I wasn't getting to see him any time soon, but maybe I could convince someone at the police station to let me have a quick word. If I told him I was trying to clear his name, I believed the vicar would tell me what he was doing at Allen's house.

I began to explain my thoughts to the team, but an interruption came in the form of a visitor ringing the front doorbell.

Like any other great house, there is a tradesman's entrance and a main reception for guests. They have distinctly different chimes. Jermaine set off without hesitation and also without hurry. It is his opinion that a butler should never need to run. That rule goes out the window when he switches into bodyguard mode, but around my house, unless armed gunmen are breaking in, he moves at a near-glacial pace.

"Where was I?" I questioned the air in general.

Barbie took a sip of her tea before supplying, "Albert was just saying that he is going to investigate the vicar and we didn't get any further than that. What are *we* going to do?"

"We're going to see Mavis." My answer wasn't the one Barbie expected. "She had a shock this morning and I want to check she is all right. Finding dead bodies might be regular for us – worryingly so – but Mavis knew Mrs Forrester and given her propensity for telling everyone everything, I worry that she might have tipped off the killer."

That hadn't occurred to anyone else. Truthfully, it had only just occurred to me, but now that the worrying thought had been aired, I needed to do something about it.

Right now, in fact.

Grabbing a sandwich from the platter, I forgave myself for the crumbs I would drop and started toward the front of the house. Talking around the delicious cheese and pickle filling, I walked backwards to talk to Albert.

"Shall we get together again later today?"

"Sounds good. Let's stay in touch with text though, keep each other updated with anything we find."

My journey from the back of the house, where the kitchen overlooks the gardens, brought me into the grand hall that sits just beyond the front entrance lobby. Expecting to find Jermaine, I was surprised to find two men bringing boxes into the house. Under Jermaine's supervision, they were making a pile to one side.

I had no idea what the boxes could contain: I hadn't ordered anything or made online purchases and my presence in England was unannounced. Of course the press knew where to find me, and my semi-celebrity status meant I was susceptible to being sent all manner of unexpected gifts.

It was none of those things.

Jermaine signed for the delivery, returning his elegant fountain pen to a pocket with a click of the lid and a flourish of his hands.

Meeting my eyes, he explained, "Personal effects from your house, madam."

Personal effects?

"Charlie had a clean out?"

"That would be my guess, madam. Would you like me to have them taken to your rooms?"

I shook my head and patted my pockets to make sure I had everything I needed. "No, sweetie, I would imagine it is all for the charity shop. This will be old clothes I no longer fit, and some other rubbish Charlie wanted out of the house."

Given how our marriage ended and the way he tried, unsuccessfully, to screw me out of the Maharaja's money, I half expected to find the boxes filled with roadkill and rotten food. Nevertheless, I could not help but wonder what might have prompted the sudden need to get his house in order.

"I believe one box has never been opened, madam," Jermaine advised in a tone that was intended not to sound curious about the box's contents yet failed in any way to do so. It worked too because he made me want to see it.

"Never opened? How can that be the case?" asked Barbie. Like me she thought the boxes were old things I'd left behind when I fled the house.

Jermaine pointed to the box in question. It was smaller than the others at roughly twelve inches square and six inches deep. It was also addressed to me at my old house with a post date of more than two months ago. Charlie had been holding it all this time and must have known I was home from chatter in the village.

Albert cleared his throat to get my attention. "I'll get going," he said when I looked up. "Much to do and the days are too short to be wasting daylight."

I wished him luck, gave Rex another pat, and once Jermaine had let them out, I turned my attention back to the box.

"Any idea what's in it?" asked Barbie.

I grabbed the box, lifting it from the floor to place it on top of the stack. "Only one way to find out."

I had it open moments later, but whatever I expected to find inside, it wasn't a bundle of old journals and a letter. The letter, like the box, was addressed to me.

The Letter

I turned it over in my hands to find the sender had included their details on the reverse as I would have. It told me two things: that the person sending the letter was of a certain age. The art of writing letters had fallen woefully by the wayside in my life. Also, the name provided, J. White, was one I knew.

Joan White is a distant relative; one I hadn't seen or thought about in many decades. In fact, if pushed to guess, I would say it had to be more than forty years since I was last in her company.

She was old back then, at least to me she was, though to be fair she was probably about the same age forty years ago as I am now. Joan was my mother's aunt, and I used the past tense for the box and the letter suggested she had recently passed.

Barbie's impatience reached its limit. "Patty can you please open it!" she squawked. "I know it's addressed to you and the contents are private and personal, but you have a secret box with old journals and a letter. If we were talking about anyone else that would be as dull as dishwater. Since they are addressed to you this has to be a big mystery for you to solve!"

Tempted to draw out her misery by placing the unopened letter back in the box until later, my own curiosity won the day.

I tore along the edge of the envelope and from inside extracted a single piece of quality writing paper.

Dear Patricia,

I hope that you remember your great aunt. I had hoped that we might be able to meet once more, but the doctors assure me I have very little time left. I hope that you will forgive me for revealing such a surprising family secret through the post.

I read the first paragraph with my eyes widening. I never had a lot of family. An only child, I lost my parents one after the other in my late twenties, and between them only my mother had a sibling, a sister from whom she was estranged.

Pressing on, I read the next part.

It was never my intention to share these journals with anyone, and it is only due to the recent developments in your life that I send them to you now. The papers report that you are a sleuth with extraordinary talent, and I read with great interest the stories of your time in Zangrabar and how you were able to topple the world's largest organised criminal group.

You may wonder where your surprising skills come from, so let me supply you with an answer: my mother was also a sleuth.

Barbie and Jermaine were keeping a respectful distance; letting me read the letter for myself while probably hoping I would reveal the content when I was ready. However, when I gasped, Barbie's feet twitched in her desperate need to know more.

"Come on," I encouraged them both. "You need to read this."

With them crowding in either side of me to start at the top, I pushed on.

Sylvia Dark, for that was my mother's maiden name, spent many years working alongside the police and taking private clients before she met my father. Parenthood forced her to stop, but as you will read in her journals, she enjoyed many exciting years investigating all manner of cases. From murderers to kidnappers, from art thieves to forgers, my mother solved crime after crime, mystery after mystery, but all without gaining the fame you managed to accrue in a fraction of the time. I guess that is how the modern world works.

I hope you enjoy discovering her adventures and that you can see in yourself a reflection of her.

Joan

I waited for my friends to catch up, watching until their eyes left the page.

Barbie was the first to speak. "Patty, this is incredible."

It truly was.

Jermaine asked, "Had you any idea, madam?"

I shook my head, feeling adrift on a cloud of conflicting emotion. "No. None at all."

Barbie moved toward the box that still held the old, leather-bound journals. "Is it ok if I have a look?"

I checked my watch. We really needed to be going. Like Albert pointed out, the days are short at this time of the year and there was much to do. Regardless, I wanted to take a peek at the words of a woman whose life must have been so much like mine for a time.

Reaching into the box, I removed the first book. It was in surprisingly good condition given that it had to be something close to a hundred years old. The spine was intact which told me few people, if any, had ever read it with the exception of my great aunt.

Carefully turning the page and questioning if I ought to be wearing white cotton gloves like a librarian might if handling a delicate and important publication, I aimed my eyes at the date in the corner.

June 3rd, 1923.

It really was a century ago.

Reading over my shoulder, Barbie said, "The Case of the Broken Vase? That doesn't sound all that interesting. I mean, is she trying to figure out who broke the vase?"

I seriously doubted it, but feeling myself getting sucked into the story, I slammed the journal shut with a dramatic motion. It made Barbie jump back out of the way.

"We need to go to the post office," I reminded her. "If we start reading that, we might still be here in the morning. The vicar needs us to clear his name, I need to make sure Mavis isn't going to get murdered, and Albert is expecting us to do our half of the investigative work."

"Spoil sport," Barbie teased.

We hurried back through the house to the garage where we clambered into the Range Rover once more. There was a mystery to solve, so while I was super keen to read more about my distant relative, it was time to get my nose to the ground.

Parish Discrepancy

- -

A lbert believed the best person to speak to was the vicar's wife. He doubted, however, that she would be available for questioning or in any state to answer.

Instead, he walked Rex back to his house. At least that's where Rex thought they were going until his human crossed the road at the last moment.

"*We're going to see Roy and Beverly?*" he asked.

Albert noted the noise Rex made and ruffled the fur around his neck as they walked side by side down his neighbour's drive. Roy was in the living room which looked out over the house's front garden and so saw his friend approaching.

He waved through the window and called to his wife on his way to answer the door.

"Hello, old boy. Solved the case yet?"

Albert scraped his feet on the doormat outside and again when he stepped inside before removing his shoes and setting them to one side on a small rack intended for precisely that use – Beverly did not like outdoor footwear on her carpets.

Standing up again, he said, "Not exactly," then proceeded to explain about the vicar's arrest, Beryl Forrester's death, and the appearance of Patricia Fisher.

"But you think Beryl was killed because of something she saw?" Beverly pushed to confirm.

Albert pursed his lips and shrugged. "Impossible to tell, but I believe she reported seeing a woman leaving Allen's house the night he was killed. She told Mavis ..."

"Which means everyone knows," Beverly concluded.

"Unfortunately, yes. Patricia was heading for the post office to narrow down who she actually told. It might be possible to generate a list of likely suspects, but given the village gossip mill, if one person knew then half of them did."

"So how can we help, old boy?" Roy steered the conversation back to a useful topic.

"Shall we sit?" suggested Beverly. "I could do with a cup of tea."

"*And biscuits,*" Rex voiced his thoughts on the subject.

Around the table, Rex sullenly sulking at the lack of food treats coming his way, Albert asked his first question.

"How long has the current vicar been with us?" He believed it was around five years, but wasn't prepared to trust himself. The amount of time might not be important, but it was always best to get these things right.

"Five years," supplied Beverly without needing to think. "The last one, Reverend Geoffrey, left while you were away, Albert Actually, thinking about when Reverend David arrived, which was in the summer, I suppose it is five and half years nearly if you want to be accurate."

Albert flicked his eyes to Roy for confirmation though he had no reason to doubt Beverly's accuracy.

Roy snorted, "Don't ask me, old boy. I go to church, but I didn't know there was going to be a test."

Aiming his questions firmly at Beverly now, Albert asked, "Do you recall where he came from? Which parish, I mean."

Beverly's brow knitted. "I know this, but I cannot recall the answer. Let me send a text to Audrey." She collected her phone from her handbag by the front door and returned to the kitchen table, her thumbs a blur of motion across her phone.

"Next question," Albert cued, "Do either of you know anything about the church's funds? Its bank accounts?"

The couple looked at each other, each searching to see if their partner could answer.

"Not really," said Beverly after a moment. "That was all managed by Allen. You don't think Allen was killed over money, do you? The church didn't have a lot of it, I shouldn't think."

Her response was what Albert expected. Churches have enough money from weekly donations to keep the lights on and that's about it. He was wrong though, a quick internet search revealed. The 'church' as a whole owns a lot of land, much of which is rented out for various uses. People pay for weddings and funerals, groups hire halls, and the church receives generous donations through wills as well as other sponsorship.

All in all it sounded as though the average church had access to substantial sums. That altered the way Albert viewed the case.

"The vicar's wife questioned what he needed the money for, and his response was not to deny taking it. That doesn't mean he did," Albert added quickly upon seeing the horrified look on Beverly's face, "but we need to keep in mind that he may have. It would explain why he was in Allen's house late last night: he was looking to find the books that show the discrepancy."

"Well, I never," murmured Roy.

Beverly's phone buzzed and beeped with an incoming text message.

"It's Audrey," she let the men know.

Albert and Roy were silent, watching her eyes skip across the screen until she said, "He came from Dover where he was a parish vicar." Her face was filled with question, so much so that Albert and Roy stayed quiet to hear what she might say next.

When she was still staring at her phone twenty seconds later, Roy touched her arm.

"What is it, dear?"

Perplexed, Beverly set her phone down. "Well, it's odd."

"What is?"

"That he was a vicar in Dover. Normally, a person studies theology because they want to take the cloth and be a priest. They qualify and get ordained by the bishop at which point they become a deacon. This period is called a curacy and it's where a young priest will learn from someone more experienced. They have to do this for a few years before they can apply to get their own parish."

"Ok," Roy pressed his wife to make a point. "So what, love. Where is the odd bit?"

"Well, he clearly went through his curacy and got a church of his own. The one in Dover. That ought to have been it. Vicars don't normally move unless they show particular talent and rise through the ranks of the church, or some other demand sends them to a new parish. They retire at seventy and move into other roles, but Reverend David moved just five years ago when he was in his early thirties, and he came from being a parish vicar to being the underling or second to a seasoned vicar here."

Albert picked up where Beverly's thoughts were going.

"Something moved him. Some circumstance meant he had to leave his parish and come here where he was essentially demoted and had to be watched over by another priest."

Beverly nodded. "Well, that's one possibility. It could be that he requested a transfer to this parish, and he then had to wait for Geoffrey to retire. Maybe it took longer than David expected for Geofrey to finally hand over the reins."

"Or it could be something insidious," Albert silenced the room.

In the corner of the room, a carriage clock ticked. It was the only sound until Roy asked, "Road trip?"

What Mavis Knew

"**M**rs Fisher. I wondered how long it would be before you came back," sighed Mavis. "Come to make a point, have you?"

I frowned and Barbie asked, "What is she talking about, Patty?"

"I don't know. What are you talking about, Mavis? What point would I have to make?"

In all my time, I have never known Mavis not to have a devilish glint in her eye and a knowing smile fixed upon her lips. She has always prided herself as the centre of village gossip and is never far from cackling about the juicy bits of news she has to share.

In contrast, her face was pale, and she looked defeated by life. It was quite the switch from how she looked this morning.

"That Beryl is dead because of me," Mavis sighed again.

My eyebrows took an upward hike of their own accord, settling back to their usual positions a moment later when I realised what Mavis was saying.

"You didn't get her killed, Mavis," I soothed. She needed a hug, but the protective Perspex barrier keeping the post office safe prevented me from coming closer. "If it were not for you, we wouldn't know what happened to her."

"But I'm the one who told people what she'd seen. They would all have told other people and one of them must have passed the message to the killer." Her voice wobbled more and more as she went on and was almost a wail by the time she finished speaking.

"But she told you willingly, Mavis, and you don't know who else she told." That placated her somewhat, and the first hint of relief showed in Mavis's eyes. "It would really help us if you could give us a list of everyone *you* told."

"Ooh, that's going to be quite the list, ladies."

No surprise there; Mavis loved to talk.

"Also, I would really like to know exactly what Beryl said. Her exact words. It could be really important."

"Ah, well, I always remembers best when I am sitting down and relaxed."

I read between the lines and said, "How about with a nice gin and tonic at the pub, Mavis? Would that help you to feel suitably relaxed?"

Mavis grinned devilishly. "You know, I think it might." Her apron was off half a second later, the post abandoned for the second time today as she headed out through the side door to arrive in the shop. "Tina, I'm going home early on account of how traumatised I am."

If Sharon cared, she showed no sign and barely acknowledged us as we left the shop.

Barbie hissed at me, "Daytime drinking is not for winners, Patty."

I shrugged. "We can both abstain, Barbie, but if gin is what is needed to pry details from Mavis, then there will be gin."

Oh, no, poor me.

Ten minutes later, with sparkling mineral water for Barbie and Jermaine, plus two industrial strength gin and tonics for me and Mavis, I pressed her to spill the beans.

She started with a list of the names of people she could recall telling about what Mrs Forrester saw. It was a long list. Too long to be helpful. If we assumed each person had told at least one other it accounted for about a third of the village.

Putting the list of names to one side, I asked Mavis about Beryl's report again.

"Well," Mavis gulped about half her gin and tonic in one go and set what was left back on the table. "She told me that she was just going to bed when the motion activated light came on above Allen's door. I think she said she was pulling her curtains at the time."

"What time was it?" I didn't really want to interrupt her flow, but the time could be important.

"Oh, um, she didn't say but I think she goes to bed quite early, so it was maybe around nine."

"Okay. Please continue."

Mavis took another swig of her drink, all but emptying it this time.

"Beryl told me she was surprised to see anyone leaving Allen's house so late because he rarely has guests. As you know he's got no family in the village, only an uncle who lives up in Aberdeen and I'm not sure when they last saw each other. Anyway, Beryl said she watched to see who it was, just out of curiosity like, and told me it was definitely a woman. She said she was dressed in black, but she didn't get a good enough look at who it was because she'd already taken off her glasses to go to bed."

That Beryl saw a woman dressed all in black didn't really tell me anything except that the killer wasn't a man.

"Did she note anything else about her features?" I coaxed Mavis for a little more detail. "Height, hair colour? Hair style? Glasses? Anything that might help to identify the person we are looking for?"

Mavis downed the dregs of her glass and indicated to Archie the barman to make another.

"Mavis," I prompted.

She twitched her head and eyes around to meet mine and scratched at the side of her face in thought. "I don't think so. I don't recall Beryl saying anything other than it was a woman in black."

The only saving grace was that the vicar didn't appear on the list of people Mavis informed after she heard the snippet of news. His wife did though, so she could easily have dropped it into conversation with her husband.

Was the vicar really behind two murders? Albert said there was a money issue behind it all and the reverend's behaviour upheld that belief.

Reaching a dead end here, the next sensible step was to visit the vicar. However, remanded into custody and almost certainly being either interviewed or briefed by his solicitor, I wasn't going to get to see him just yet. Not that it wasn't worth a try and the nick in Maidstone isn't that far to go.

If I couldn't get to him, perhaps I would be able to confirm where I might find his wife. She had to know more about the situation than anyone else. Perhaps she knew all about the money and why the vicar took it.

I thanked Mavis for her time and paid for the drinks. It was already mid-afternoon, and the light would begin to dwindle soon. If we were going to achieve anything today, we needed to get moving.

Case Closed

P arking at the police station in Maidstone is easy enough at the right time of day. This wasn't it. However, it was simple enough to park in one of the many public carparks and walk the rest of the way so that was what we did.

I was recognised coming through the door, the duty sergeant at the reception desk and the young constable working with him both looked up when the door opened. The sergeant looked down again, his attention on his current task until his brain caught up.

"Mrs Fisher," he almost blurted, the tone of his voice betraying surprise and excitement while explaining the doubletake.

I guess being quasi-famous has its perks because I got to tell him what I needed without a longwinded explanation regarding why.

"The suspect in the double homicide?" He winced. "Ooh, I don't think I will be able to get you in to see him. In fact, I think the chief inspector is interviewing him as we speak. Do you want me to see if he's done? Or find out if he wants your help?"

Barbie snorted a laugh.

Ignoring her, I said, "No, thank you." I guess the gossip mill in the nick hadn't picked up the nature of my relationship with Chief Inspector Quinn. "Will it be possible to see Reverend David Gentry later, do you imagine?"

The sergeant pulled an apologetic expression. "Hard to say, Mrs Fisher. A lot depends on whether he confesses or not."

The constable piped up, "I heard he was still denying the charges."

Refusing to confess would not prevent Quinn from pressing charges. If the Crown Prosecution Service could be convinced there was enough evidence to be sure they had the right person and that a conviction could be achieved, the vicar could go all the way to sentencing without admitting he did it.

While this was troubling, it was hardly unexpected. Even if we were not talking about Chief Inspector Quinn, any other officer in charge would be pushing to get a confession. Taken at face value, the evidence collated thus far all pointed toward the vicar. However, to me, that just meant we were missing a lot of puzzle pieces.

With a thank you to the sergeant for his excellent work, a remark that made him beam with pride – always good to have a few police officers on one's side – I led my party back to the car. The sun was falling now, the light running for the horizon, though with the tall buildings of the city reflecting the sun's rays back down, it was artificially bright where we stood.

A few minutes later, and heading back to more rural settings, the streetlights were already on. The trees were completely naked, their leaves having fallen weeks ago and the hedgerows, which must have teemed with greenery until recently, were nothing more than interwoven twigs now. In the distance, the rolling hills of the North Downs, a series of humps that undulate through Kent, showed as black mounds looming over the land.

One positive was that we could see the lights were on inside the vicarage when we pulled up outside it. Jermaine parked in the street rather than on the driveway and the three of us approached the house together.

The vicar and his wife were still childless, and I could not say whether that was due to conscious decision, a lack of trying, or fertility issues. Nor was it any of my business nor germane to the case. What it did mean was that the lights inside almost certainly meant the vicar's wife was home.

Hopefully, she was home alone as quizzing her would be easier that way.

Jermaine pressed the door buzzer, the chime inside the house ringing loud enough for us to hear outside. A shadow at the window to our right revealed the vicar's wife looking out to see who was there.

She had her phone to one ear and appeared deep in conversation. She also looked much as she always did which relieved me. I half expected her makeup to be a tear-streaked mess, the impact of her husband's arrest leaving her emotionally unable to cope with my desire to question her.

Her faced pinched upon seeing who was at her door, but only for a moment. She moved away from the window, undoubtedly on her way to let us in and had to have wrapped her call up quickly because her phone was gone when she opened the door ten seconds later.

"Patricia." She beamed radiantly, overcompensating. "Are you here because you have heard?"

She didn't clarify what she was talking about and there was no need to.

With a heartfelt and apologetic nod, I said, "Yes. That, of course, is why we are here. Can we come in?"

The vicar's wife took a step back, holding the door as we filed inside.

"You've met Barbie and Jermaine?" I sought to confirm. They both accompanied me to church in the brief period when we lived in the village, and I knew their faces must be familiar.

Sadie held out her hand to Barbie. "I don't think we've ever actually met. I'm Sadie."

"Barbie."

"That's a fun name."

"And this is Jermaine," I introduced my butler who dipped his head graciously when he accepted Sadie's hand to shake.

"I'll not beat around the bush, Sadie." She was leading us through the vicarage to the living room and I was talking to the back of her head. "I want to prove your husband's innocence and I intend to do so as swiftly as possible."

I was about to say I would need her help to do that which would lead nicely into a whole bunch of questions. However, I didn't get that far because the vicar's wife said something I wasn't expecting.

"I think that might be a waste of your time, Patricia."

Entering the living room, Sadie turned to face me, and we all stopped moving.

A tear slipped from her right eye; the first show of emotion and an indication of how she was really feeling despite her brave face. She tipped her head back and wiped at it with an annoyed hand.

"Please, excuse me. This day has been rather trying."

All three of us made placating sounds – she was perfectly within her rights to be tearful.

Gathering herself, Sadie stalked across the room to a cabinet. There she opened a flap to reveal bottles and glasses, including a selection of gins I tried very hard not to notice. Without touching any of them, she spun on her heels to face us again.

"You will want to know what I meant by my last comment."

I really did.

"I believe, and believe me it pains me to say this, but I believe my husband is more than likely guilty."

"Of murdering two people?" I gasped, shocked that the vicar's wife could think such a thing.

Sadie slumped a little, one hand gripping the cabinet as if for support.

"Sorry," she murmured again. "I've spent most of the day talking to the police. I've only been home a few minutes. They had all manner of questions for me, and they ripped right through the house looking for evidence. I feel ... violated, I guess," she managed to articulate her feelings. "Do you mind if I get a drink?"

"No, of course," I encouraged, my own lips eager to taste a drop from the bottle of Hendricks I could see. So it wasn't my first drink of the day; investigating is thirsty work. "Why don't you take a seat. Jermaine will make you something, won't you, sweetie?"

Jermaine was already moving in the direction of the drinks' cabinet.

"It would be my pleasure, madam."

To the sound of clinking glasses and glugging liquids I pressed the vicar's wife to explain why she thought her husband could have killed two people.

"The police have all the evidence," she replied, her eyes cast down at the carpet.

I couldn't claim to know the woman well, but she possessed a confident radiance that lit up rooms when she entered them. In stark contrast, she was curled into a tight ball in one corner of her sofa, her feet tucked under her body. I would call the look bedraggled were she not so dry.

"They asked me about specific times. They wanted to know where he was and if he was at home. I had to tell them he was out, and I guess the times corresponded with the murders because the chief inspector seemed very happy with my answers."

I bet he did.

"They asked me about money too. We've never really had any, though David hides that well. Honestly, I don't know where it all goes, but we are short every month. The police said they found David's prints in Allen's house and on the knife they found sticking out of his back." Sadie let out a small sob at that point and needed a minute and a good swig of gin before she could continue. "It was our knife from our kitchen!" She needed a moment to compose herself, the rest of us staying silent while she blew her nose and tussled with her emotions.

Ready to speak again, Sadie took a mouthful of gin and shuddered before picking up where she left off.

"He embezzled thousands from the church roof fund; they showed me the proof. It was all in the treasurer's ledger."

I had so many questions boiling in my head, but I held my tongue to let Sadie talk.

"They had a fight a few days ago. I don't think I was supposed to hear it. I came back from bell ringing practice and there was shouting coming from the pantry. I listened – I know that's a bad thing to do, but I couldn't help myself. David was shouting and I wasn't sure who the other voice belonged to until the door slammed and I saw Allen storming across our lawn."

"What were they saying?" I wanted to know the details of their argument.

Sadie hadn't looked up in the last five minutes and nothing changed when she said, her voice as quiet as a mouse's, "Sorry. I couldn't make out the words. They were shouting, but through the pantry door it was too muffled to understand. I probably should have gone closer, but I didn't want to be caught eavesdropping if David suddenly came back into the kitchen."

We chatted for a little longer, but my steam had well and truly run out and I was only hanging around because I didn't want the tearful vicar's wife to be left alone. Mercifully, I was rescued from my sense of duty by the arrival of two of Sadie's friends. Apparently, they knew each other from Uni and the girls had dropped everything to come to their friend's aid.

Retreating to the door while her friends were still taking off their coats, we bade our best wishes and escaped.

"What now, Patty?" asked Barbie when we were at the car. "Is that case closed?"

Was it? I couldn't get my head around the vicar being the killer. It just felt ... wrong. However, from an evidence point of view, I had to admit the case against Reverend David looked watertight.

With a sigh I said, "Dinner, Barbie. That's what is next. I shall call Albert and see how he got on, but unless he has something startling to tell us, I rather think this could be, as you said, case closed."

Dead Ends

B everly parked her E Class Mercedes in a visitor's spot next to a bright yellow Toyota Aygo, a tiny car that looked light and flimsy enough that a decent gust of wind might blow it over. They were outside St Francis Church in Kingsdown, a suburb of Dover where a series of phone calls made in the car resulted in the current vicar agreeing to meet them.

Albert wasn't coy regarding the reason for their interest, though he skirted the truth about Reverend David Gentry's current predicament. Rather than reveal he had been arrested a few hours ago – news would not have travelled that fast, Albert felt certain – he claimed to need to know why the East Malling parish vicar left Dover so suddenly. In posing the question in such a way, the response confirmed there was a reason behind the move, just as Beverly suggested there must be.

Reverend Wendy Mallas could have said she didn't know why her predecessor moved, or could have provided an explanation that proved to be completely benign. She did neither thing. Instead, she was silent for a beat after Albert made his request to speak with her, then calmly advised she would meet him at the church. Not the vicarage where she might have family, and ears could overhear, but at a secluded building where Albert and his friends knew no one else would be about.

"I guess that must be her car," said Roy, looking at the yellow Toyota.

Rex sat up to look out the window. He'd spent the journey stretched out asleep across the back seat with his jaw resting on his human's right leg. Now he was awake and in need of an outhouse.

He made a whimpering sound and nudged the door.

Understanding his dog well enough to know what he needed, Albert said, "Rex will need a minute. I'll take him for a walk around the grounds."

"Not sure you'll get the chance, old boy." Albert looked where Roy was now pointing – at the entrance to the church where a tall, thin woman was heading their way. She had a thick, burgundy winter coat over her clothes, the top snap unbuttoned to show her dog collar. The rest of the clothes were black and there was no mistaking that they were looking at a vicar.

It wasn't Reverend Wendy though, as they soon discovered.

"Archdeacon Janice Dock," she shook hands and introduced herself. "And you are Albert Smith. I recognise you from the television."

"Yes," said Albert, unhappy as always to be so well known.

"You have some questions for me, I believe," The archdeacon got straight to the point. "Shall we go inside?"

"Ooh, yes," said Beverly. "I love looking around old churches. They are such romantic places, don't you think?"

The archdeacon arched an eyebrow. "I'm not sure romantic is the term I would reach for first."

"Oh, I just mean they are filled with the wonder of Christ, and they are placed where families can come together, that kind of romantic, not the other kind."

Trying to get his wife off the subject, Roy gave her a shove to get moving. "Come along, love, it's cold outside."

"Don't you be pushing me, Wing Commander. I shall jolly well push you back."

Albert rolled his eyes and went around them.

"No dogs inside, thank you," intoned the archdeacon in a voice that held no room for discussion.

Rex was holding back anyway, still in need of a place to do his business.

"I'll ... um. I'll meet you inside in a minute," Albert offered.

Rex didn't need long, just enough time to find the right spot. Off the lead and free to roam – vastly superior to having his human standing next to him – Rex wandered the churchyard. There were odd squares of stone on the ground in places and some of them were arranged to stick straight up into the air.

Rex went to lift a leg against one only to have his human grab his collar and haul him away from it.

"*What's with you?*" Rex asked. "*I'm outside. It's an inanimate object. That's within the rules, isn't it?*"

"That's a grave, Rex," Albert attempted to explain. "Go pee somewhere else."

Rex's brow performed a little dance. Had there been a murder? If the stone marked someone's grave ... there were so many of them in one place. What did that mean?

Perplexed, but with a pressing need that had to come first, Rex put the worrying questions about the graves to one side. When he was done, his human urging him to hurry up, he found himself clipped back to his lead and then attached to the railing at the edge of the churchyard.

He got a pat on the head and a promise his human wouldn't be too long. Rex watched Albert depart with a frown. 'Too long' had no meaning. All he knew was that his human was gone, and he was stuck waiting for the old man to reappear when he could be doing something more interesting.

For once, Rex was quite confused about what they were doing. He thought they were trying to catch a killer, but also believed the vicar had something to do with it. He chased him from the house where a body had most definitely been and then saw him being taken away by the police.

To Rex's mind that ought to be the end of it, but listening to the humans talk, they were clearly still pursuing evidence.

Rex settled onto the grass, resting his head on his front paws to think.

Inside the church, Albert had found the archdeacon and his friends only a few yards from the door – that was as far as they had gone.

"Are we learning anything?" he asked.

The question was aimed at Roy and Beverly, but it was the archdeacon who chose to answer.

"I'm afraid there is nothing much to learn, Mr Smith."

Roy explained, "It would seem the vicar chose to leave of his own accord."

"Is that unusual?" Albert switched into a detective's role instantly.

The archdeacon smiled innocently. "The clergy move about all the time. Their reasons for doing so can be as plentiful as the fish in the sea."

"What was *his* reason?" Albert pressed, watching the archdeacon to see how she would react.

Her smile held, but only on her mouth. The warmth in her eyes dimmed and they narrowed ever so slightly.

However, she replied almost without hesitation, "I believe it was for love, Mr Smith. David met his wife and they moved to a parish closer to her home and family. Beyond that, I cannot provide any further explanation, though I am sure the vicar or his wife will be able to do so." Fixing Albert with a harder gaze, she asked, "I am curious to know why you are so interested in your parish vicar's past."

Since it was a statement and not a question, Albert saw no reason to provide an answer. Instead, he said, "Were there any suggestions of financial impropriety during his tenure here?"

The archdeacon's eyes flared in surprise.

"Goodness me, no. Whatever would make you ask such a question?" She gave a small gasp, sensing the source of the enquiry. "Is that what this is about? Is there some issue at your parish? You cannot surely believe David could be responsible for any missing money."

Roy cut his eyes at Albert for confirmation before revealing the truth.

"Reverend David was arrested this morning."

The archdeacon rocked in place as though buffeted by a stiff breeze.

Her jaw dropping, she asked, "For embezzlement?"

Albert gave a half shrug of apology before delivering, "For double homicide."

"Whoa here," Roy moved to catch the archdeacon when she looked like she might faint.

Sounding even more apologetic Albert explained how they hoped he was innocent and that they were actively engaged in trying to prove it one way or the other.

Roy and Beverly helped the archdeacon to a pew.

"Can I get you some tea?" Bevely asked.

"Tea? No." The archdeacon reached inside her coat, producing a hip flask much to everyone's surprise. "I keep this for those occasions when I must deal with bereavements. They always leave me feeling washed out and there's nothing like a nip of the good stuff to put a spring back in one's step."

She offered the hipflask to her guests who all chose to decline. They hung around until they could be sure the archdeacon was safe to be left and hadn't imbibed so much of 'the good stuff' that she wouldn't be able to drive. Ultimately though, they were looking to leave.

The trip wasn't necessarily wasted, but it sure felt like the sum of their achievements was close to nil.

Reverend David chose to leave Dover to make his wife's life easier.

Albert almost bade goodbye and thanked the archdeacon, but he couldn't avoid wanting to know why he was talking to her and not the vicar for the parish to whom he had spoken not more than thirty minutes earlier.

"Because she called me on the matter," the archdeacon replied. "Reverend Wendy Mallas arrived after David left and thus is poorly placed to answer any questions about the circumstances regarding his move from this parish to yours."

"And you just happened to be available?" Albert made sure to keep the accusation from his tone, but the question was a challenge, nevertheless.

The archdeacon frowned when she replied, "I work in the offices of the Bishop of Dover less than ten minutes' drive from here. You should also know that David was my deacon when he left theology school and moved into the church. I know him better than almost anyone."

Satisfied with her answers, Albert pulled his coat tighter and thanked the archdeacon for her candour.

Rex lifted his head when the church door opened, his hopeful eyes searching for his human. Upon seeing the old man exit first, Rex clambered to his feet, stretched, and yawned. He'd had a very short nap and was ready for a proper sleep now. Were they going back in the car?

The humans were talking, discussing something though Rex could not hear what it was. Wagging his tail when his human angled his feet in Rex's direction, he watched Beverly open the car and get in.

"Okay, Rex?" Albert asked. "That wasn't too long, was it?"

Time, too long or too short, were all inconceivable concepts to Rex, just as they were to all other dogs, but he could understand that his human was showing concern, so he licked his hand and trotted gamely back to the car where he settled contentedly back in the same position he'd occupied on the drive down.

Rex was just dozing off when the car began to move, the humans talking again.

"Home for dinner, is it?" Beverly asked.

Albert nodded, his attention on the darkness beyond his window. "Yes, I think so." However, inside his head, Albert supposed he wanted to find out if Patricia and her cohort had better luck with their side of the investigation.

He would get Beverly to drop him in the village and his meandering route home could take him by her residence.

Sinking into his seat, his head against the headrest, it wasn't long before Albert joined his lightly snoring dog.

There's Somebody at the Door

"**M**ay I take your plate, madam?" Jermaine hovered next to me.

"Of course, sweetie," I replied, sighing internally for he was now to tackle the dishes and would not allow me to assist. "Thank you for dinner. It was delicious."

"And it was macro balanced," cheered Barbie, happy to sneak in another meal that was high in protein, low in fat, and helped to make sure I kept within my daily calorie allowance.

I love them both dearly but have regular urges to murder them in their sleep.

A ring from the front doorbell echoed through the house. I was not expecting any guests and was yet to hear from Albert – I planned to call him for a catch up after dinner, but the caller could be anyone and so long as it wasn't another reporter hoping for an exclusive, I was ready to welcome them in.

Jermaine dried his hands on a towel before butlering slowly through the house.

I followed, keeping ten paces behind so I could see who it was and save Jermaine the slow trip back to report my visitor's identity.

A little inkling told me it was going to be Albert and I was pleased to hear that I was right when his dulcet tones met my ears.

"Do come in," I called, quickening my pace to catch up with Jermaine. He was already inviting Albert across the threshold, Rex coming first and pulling on his lead to get inside.

"Hello, Rex," I ruffled the fur around his neck to the beat of his wagging tail. "How did today go?"

My question was aimed at Albert, not Rex.

Albert shucked his coat, letting Jermaine take it before saying, "Took a trip to Dover with Roy Hope and his wife. The vicar ministered to a parish there before he came here. We thought there might be something in that, but we met with an archdeacon who assured us nothing untoward occurred prior to his early departure from that parish. According to her, he left ..." Albert's phone began to ring and he looked about his person for it. "Sorry, according to her ... where is the blasted thing?"

"Here, sir," Jermaine fished it from Albert's coat which was still draped over his arm.

Albert nodded his thanks, turning the phone the right way around to read the screen.

"Roy already? I'll call him back. Now where was I?"

"The archdeacon," Barbie prompted.

"Ah, yes. The archdeacon told us the vicar left for love. He was getting married and moved from his parish to this one so his wife could stay close to her family."

The back of my head itched.

I was about to question why when Albert's phone started to ring again.

"Goodness me," he sighed, but this time the caller wasn't Roy, it was Greta Hill. I spotted the name even though I didn't intend to look. Questioning what she might want, I guess, he answered the call by tapping the green button, but before he could get it to his ear a second call buzzed in. Albert sure was popular for some reason.

"Roy again," he remarked, letting me know the identity of his second caller, though whether he did so intentionally or not, I can only speculate.

Speaking into his phone, though his eyes stayed on me, Albert said, "Greta, dear, is everything all right?"

Jermaine busied himself hanging Albert's coat and I backed away, providing him with a modicum of privacy. Albert clicked his fingers at me though, gesticulating that I should be involved though he had not placed the call on speaker.

"Really?" he asked, confirming whatever it was Greta just said to him. "Just now?" He spoke then paused, listening to Greta before speaking again. "Goodness, no, Greta. Do not go yourself! I'm with Patricia."

A pause.

"Yes, Greta, Patricia Fisher."

A pause.

"Yes, her giant butler is with me too. We will leave right away. There's little point calling the police. It will all be over long before they arrive."

My curiosity, which admittedly runs high all the time anyway, was currently demanding I poke Albert with something pointy. I wanted to know what was going on and what would all be over by the time we got there and where exactly 'there' was in the first place.

"We're leaving now," Albert assured Greta to end the call.

Jermaine held Albert's coat once more, opened and ready for Albert to slide his arms in.

Still holding his phone, he did just that, but finally filled in the blanks.

"There's someone snooping around the church. Greta is ..."

"Second in Command of the Neighbourhood Watch for the village. Yes, I know." Greta meant well but was known to overreact. I once heard that she had the local constabulary out to investigate burglars only to discover the sound of moving furniture coming from her neighbour's house was the occupant snoring.

Albert acknowledged my point without me needing to make it, but said, "Greta said the lights outside came on and then went off again and that she saw a figure merge into the darkness by the vestry door. The church council are due to meet there in an hour to discuss what they do about the vicar now that he is in jail."

"He's not actually in jail," I pointed out.

Albert rolled his eyes and smiled. "You and I both know how the custodial process goes, but for the layperson, locked up at the local nick is the same thing. Anyway, if there is someone trying to break in, I would like to catch them in the act. Do you wish to accompany me?"

Jermaine made eye contact with me, his intentions clear. He is not the sort of person who lets another person face potential danger alone. Even if alone in Albert's case means armed with an oversized German Shepherd dog.

Rex was at the door already, his canine brain able to sense there was something going on and that he was going back out again.

I nodded, accepting my coat when Jermaine offered it.

"What's going on?" asked Barbie approaching from behind us. "Are you guys going out again?"

"There might be an intruder at the church," supplied Jermaine, donning his bowler hat, and grabbing his long, black umbrella with a sense of purpose.

"Well, you're not leaving me here," insisted our blonde friend, dashing forward to join us.

Together, we barrelled out of the door and into the night, opting to walk the quarter mile to the church so we could approach in a stealthy manner.

As soon as we drew close, I could see Albert was having to battle Rex. The dog was straining at his lead, his nose twitching and snorting as though he had caught a familiar scent.

A Familiar Scent

"**I** *know who that is*," barked Rex, straining to set free.

Albert tensed, leaning back to hold on to his dog.

Next to him, Jermaine used an arm as a barrier to allay my forward movement and doffed his hat. Handing it backward without looking, his eyes were focused on the darkness around the church when Barbie accepted it silently.

I whispered, "I don't see anyone."

Albert, a small grin teasing one corner of his mouth returned, "Well, if you can see 'em, they ain't Apaches."

Barbie said, "Huh?" her brow wrinkling in confusion.

"John Wayne quotes, Albert?" I sighed, the light-heartedness of the moment fading fast when everyone saw a shadow move.

Jermaine started forward.

I reached after him instinctively, but closed my fingers before they could grip his jacket. Instead of trying to stop him, I hissed, "Be careful, Sweetie!"

Jermaine didn't look back, and Barbie went with him, sidestepping me as she followed her friend just a couple of yards to his rear. He is the trained fighter, she is merely strong and fast, but she wasn't going to let him face danger alone, if that was what awaited him.

Rex struggled against his lead, his desire to go making his paws twitch with impatience.

I took a step toward Albert, gripping the sleeve of his coat to make sure he didn't leave me.

"Perhaps the two of us should remain here to observe," I suggested.

Rex barked, the words leaving his mouth indecipherable by everyone except the intended recipient who barked back.

"There's another dog," murmured Albert to himself. His eyes were nowhere near as sharp as they used to be, but he could still see well enough in the dark. There was someone out there. Maybe more than one someone, and they had a dog.

A canine threat added an unexpected element and the possibility of injury to Barbie and Jermaine. They might not see it coming and depending on the breed, a dog has the potential to cause terrible wounds with a single bite.

Reluctantly, Albert accepted the need to let Rex go. He was just as susceptible to wounding if he came up against a larger dog or one bred or even trained for fighting, but one of his purposes as a police dog had been to protect human life.

Unsnapping the clip on his dog's lead, Albert whispered, "Go on, boy. Sic 'em."

Ahead of Rex, I watched Jermaine and Barbie reach the edge of the church. A single lamp above the door shone down to illuminate the entrance, but the light from it was eaten by the dark before it could venture more than a few yards. They were to the right, halfway down the eastern flank of the ancient building where the trees, bushes, and gravestones absorbed even more light. On a starry night, it would be merely dark and foreboding. Under the blanket of clouds currently blotting out the moon, we might as well have been inside a bag for all I could see, and it wasn't until we heard a crunch of gravel that Barbie and Jermaine were able to orientate themselves toward the threat.

I strained to see in the cloak of inky blackness and shadow, and jolted when a head appeared from behind a gravestone. I couldn't stop myself from shouting, "Over there!" I pointed at the place where the person had just been, but I need not have bothered.

Barbie and Jermaine had spotted it too and were moving fast to intercept.

Rex, meanwhile, had belted into the depths of the churchyard, but unlike his human companions, his world was lit up as though he were wearing night vision goggles. The myriad kaleidoscope of smells clinging to every surface provided a map of the terrain only a dog's sensitive nose could read.

He knew where he needed to go and found the trail of the other dog almost instantly. Now all he had to do was follow it.

"Hey!" I heard Jermaine shout to get the person's attention before he leapt to deliver his opening salvo. On any other occasion, or under different circumstances, he might have taken a more cautious approach, yet the person he sought was wearing all black which included a head covering.

It was not a look that would inspire anyone to believe they were just out for a walk.

Ninjas in the Dark

- -

C oncerned they might be armed – likely if they were here for nefarious deeds – Jermaine called to make them look his way so he could take them down with a single hold. Not a strike, but a limb twist that would incapacitate them. In the event that the person was just an innocent, he would apologise but would not have caused them any great harm.

However, when the assailant in black shot around at the sound of his voice, they moved in a way that was completely unexpected. Dropping and rolling to get away, Jermaine watched the person convert their roll into a handspring – they pushed off the ground to flip in the air and land on their feet.

In the time it took for gravity to pull him back to Earth, Jermaine changed his strategy entirely. He wasn't dealing with a person out for a walk, and this wasn't an opportunistic criminal looking for things to steal at the church. No, this was someone with learned skill, a fighter, and that belief was confirmed a heartbeat later when he saw them pull a weapon from behind their back.

Jermaine heard Barbie gasp – she was close enough behind to see what was happening even in the dark.

Unconcerned, and wise enough not to let his opponent's move distract him, he struck out with a sweeping arm to block the weapon before it could be brought to bear. Idly, he noted it was a sai, a three-pronged martial arts weapon he'd never seen outside of a dojo.

What he failed to consider was that his opponent never intended to use it. Showing the weapon was a feint, the real play coming from the other hand which struck his throat before he could block it.

Forced back a pace, he had to defend against a flurry of blows, each as hard to see as the one before, the black clothes merged so well with the background.

Struggling to breathe after the blow to his larynx, Jermaine knew to be patient. If he gave himself a few seconds, an opening would come.

Forty yards away, Rex's nose was closing on the dog he sought. He'd heard his human call for him more than once, but chose to delay responding until he located his quarry.

Moving faster than he knew the other dog could, he darted around a gravestone and almost into Buster's cocked leg.

"*Hey, Rex!*" Buster barked, lowering his leg. "*Sorry, I was busting. They've had me in the car for ages. Said I couldn't go in the church for some reason.*"

Rex dropped into a play-bow, happy to see his friend.

"*Good to see you, Buster. My human is back this way. Where's yours?*"

Buster lifted his head, sniffing the air. "*Around here somewhere.*"

A yell echoed through the darkness, giving both dogs a direction to run which for once was easier than using their noses. They set off, wending through the graves to find the humans.

The yell had come from Jermaine's opponent when he finally found a way to land a worthwhile strike. The black-clad ninja was fast, but small, nearly half a foot shorter which gave him a reach advantage. They were slight too, their blows vicious yet lacking in power. It made Jermaine believe he might be fighting a woman.

This belief solidified a moment later when his scything foot struck the ribs on his opponent's left side, driving the air from their lungs with an accompanying cry of pain in a young woman's voice.

She staggered, but only for the briefest of moments. However, as she recovered her stance and readied to come again, Jermaine held out a hand, palm extended.

"Stop." It was a command, and his posture, now relaxed and unthreatening, caused her to comply.

Tearing off her hood, she said, "Jermaine?"

Barbie's eyes just about popped out of her head. "Mindy?"

Mindy twitched her eyes to her right, noticing the blonde for the first time.

"Yes. Mindy! Why did you attack me?"

While Barbie turned around to call for Patricia and Albert, Jermaine drew in a deep, calming breath. "I apologise. You are dressed all in black and we are investigating a double-homicide. I'm afraid I assumed you were up to no good. It was not my intention to harm you, merely subdue so *you* could do no harm. Are you okay?" he enquired, remembering her cry of pain.

Mindy touched her ribs. "I'm fine. Good hit though. Didn't see it coming in time."

Jermaine dipped his head to acknowledge her compliment. "It was hard to find an opening. You are better trained than I realised."

"Thank you." The sound of something approaching at speed through the undergrowth turned her attention to the left, but she added, as kindly as she could, "You need to work on your speed. All that muscle makes you slow."

Rex, going slow so he wouldn't leave Buster behind, burst into sight just as the moon peeked out from behind the clouds to bathe them in light.

"*Mindy!*" barked Buster. "*I found Rex! Rex is here!*"

Now that Patty and Albert were on their way, Barbie turned her attention back to Mindy.

"Why are you dressed like a ninja? And what was the weapon I saw?"

"Oh, yeah. Good point." Mindy looked around until she spotted it, and retrieving her sai from the ground she said, "I'm wearing sports clothes. The same stuff I usually wear. The top just happens to have a full hood I can pull over my face."

"Just happens to have?" Barbie questioned. "And you just happened to have it over your head while wandering around a graveyard at night."

They couldn't see it, but Mindy's cheeks were sporting a lot of colour.

"Yeah. I didn't think anyone else was about. I was pretending to be a ninja."

"What are you doing here anyway?"

"Mindy?" called a new voice, this one coming from the front of the church.

Mindy raised an arm and called, "Over here, Auntie!"

All the Gang is Here. Well, Nearly

With Albert by my side, I had almost reached Barbie and her group when light spilled from the church door and to my great surprise Felicity Philips stuck her head out. I could hear Barbie and Jermaine talking to someone, but could only guess who it was until I heard Felicity call her niece's name.

At that point I diverted my course to converge with the whole gang at the church entrance.

Handshakes were exchanged along with explanations as I had no idea Albert and Felicity knew each other.

"Felicity," I started once the catching up was done, "can I ask what you are doing here? This isn't your parish. Do you have a wedding here this weekend?"

Felicity exhaled hard, huffing in a defeated manner.

"No, I don't have a wedding here, but Miriam Merchant is getting married in a few weeks and your vicar is supposed to be conducting the ceremony."

Both Albert and I knew Miriam Merchant. A member of the village, she was marrying a tech millionaire and moving away. She was a regular at Sunday morning worship, so it came as no great surprise to hear she was borrowing 'her' vicar for the service.

Albert questioned, "You know the vicar has been arrested, yes?"

Felicity huffed again. "That's why I'm here."

The statement required at least a little more explanation though it was Mindy who supplied it.

"Auntie thinks this is the work of someone trying to mess with the royal wedding."

Albert nodded. "That's right. You're the wedding planner for Prince Marcus and his bride. I read about that. Congratulations."

Felicity managed a weak smile. "It's turning out to be a poisoned chalice."

Everyone waited for her to expand. Except Rex and Buster, that is. They were chatting in the church entrance, Buster regaling Rex with stories about visiting the palace and having to save Felicity. In turn, Rex explained about the two most recent murders in the village and how he was confused about why they were still trying to solve them.

Felicity met my eyes with an expression that could only be called 'deadly serious'.

"I think someone is trying to mess with the wedding." Taking in the cocked eyebrows and quizzical faces clearly expecting more, she said, "There have been ... incidents. Someone messaged everyone in my supply chain attempting to sever my business with them. The warehouse of the caterer I selected to supply the bulk of the ingredients for the wedding breakfast mysteriously burned down a week ago. I'm sure you heard about the spate of deaths among the upper echelons of the royal family?"

Albert pursed his lips grimly. "What's the current tally for the year?" It had been in the news recently following yet another unexpected and untimely death. They were all natural causes. Well, and a few accidents, but to his knowledge and mine there was no suspicion of foul play and no investigation looking into it.

"Fourteen." Mindy provided the number in a suitably quiet tone. "I don't think anyone knows, but it started with Eddie's brother just over a year ago. He died in a weird accident at the palace. Eddie won't talk about it, but I heard from one of the guards that he was in a dragon suit that could fly and burned to death inside it."

"A dragon suit?" repeated Jermaine, voicing the bewilderment everyone else felt.

"One moment," I raised my hand to still the others. "Who's Eddie? I feel like I have missed something important."

"Oh," Mindy smiled coyly, her cheeks burning just a little. "That's my boyfriend."

Felicity rolled her eyes. "Mindy is dating a member of the royal family."

Barbie's eyes went wide like side plates. "Way to go, girl! Is he a prince?"

"The son of a duke," Felicity replied. "He lives inside Buckingham Palace and his family have the kind of money that buys small islands."

"They have three in the Caribbean," Mindy admitted quietly.

Barbie looked like she was reconsidering how she felt about her junior doctor boyfriend.

Dismissing the line of conversation, Albert directed a question at Felicity, "Who do you think might be behind it?"

He got a shrug from Felicity in reply. "That's what I've been trying to figure out. I mean, are the royal family deaths all just unfortunate coincidences? Can they be? If there is a person behind it, is it the same person who is messing with my organisation for the royal wedding?"

"That's why you are here then," I surmised. "You think maybe the vicar's situation is another example of the same and you hoped to find a connection that would lead you to identify the person orchestrating your pain."

"That about sums it up," Felicity sighed. "I came to the church to look for clues." Her cheeks reddened a touch before she admitted, "I'm not actually sure what it is that I hoped to find."

Jermaine cleared his throat. "If I may, ladies and gentlemen. I believe we will all be more comfortable back at the residence."

I understood his suggestion. It was nothing to do with comfort, but his knowledge that I would rather do this with a glass of gin and tonic in my hand. He was one hundred percent right on that count.

We decamped, Felicity taking me, Mindy, and Buster in her car while the others walked the short cross-country distance back to my house.

There, we arranged ourselves around the kitchen table to discuss the matter further with snacks and drinks.

"Wow," gasped Mindy, swallowing her first mouthful of gin and pulling a face. "That's nice, but a bit strong."

I chuckled. "Sorry, Jermaine makes it how I like it. Just top it up with some more tonic if you want it weaker."

We exchanged what we knew which wasn't a whole lot. The vicar took money from the church roof fund; we believed that much was true. However, we did not yet know how much money or how long ago the embezzlement started. I told Albert and Felicity what Sadie said about her husband's loud verbal fight with Allen three days before he was found murdered and it seemed likely the argument was to do with the missing money.

But why did he take it in the first place? What was it for? Furthermore, as the treasurer, Allen must have known about it when it first occurred, so his interest three days ago could not have been sudden or unexpected.

All in all, everything we knew made the vicar look guilty and it was only our collective determination to believe he must be innocent that kept us talking.

"What about Mrs Forrester?" asked Barbie. "We saw her broken watch. She died at half past eight. Didn't Albert say the vicar was at a church council meeting?"

Albert shook his head. "That broke up before eight and her house is a five-minute walk from the church hall. He could have got there in time."

"That's if he left straight away," I cautioned everyone to avoid assumptions.

"That's right," agreed Albert. "But I'm sure I heard him getting ready to leave when I was going out the door with Roy."

"What about his wife?" asked Jermaine. "Could she clear this up? She was there with him, was she not?"

"She was," Albert conceded. "I guess we still have a whole bunch of loose ends to tidy before we accept defeat."

I tipped back my glass, emptying the last dregs of gin, tonic and melted ice into my mouth and tapping the bottom of the glass to encourage any final drops to volunteer themselves.

"Let's call it a night. It is getting late, and we all need some sleep. We can reconvene in the morning."

"Us too?" Felicity wanted to confirm she was invited.

"If you want to be involved," I replied, getting up. "Many hands and all that."

"We need to know more about the money," Albert stated his opinion, crossing the room to place his glass next to the sink.

Barbie said, "I think I might be able to do something about that." When Albert looked her way, she gave a little sigh and pointed to her chest. "These tend to make men want to tell me things they otherwise might not reveal."

I agreed, "They have been known to get answers when we need them."

Selecting his words with an eye on political correctness, and being sure not to stare at the subjects of the conversation, Albert said, "I dare say it's the package that get's men to talk, not just your ... um, assets."

"No, Albert, it's the boobs," Barbie chuckled. "It's always been the boobs."

Breakfast and Plans

I awoke the next morning feeling out of place. So used to waking in my cabin on board the Aurelia, even after nearly a week away from it, I was still surprised not to find myself there when my eyes opened.

Normally, there would be a small warm lump pressing against me too. Not from my boyfriend, Alistair, the captain of the ship, please get your mind out of the gutter. No, the small warm lump, or often two, would be from my mother and daughter duo of miniature dachshunds. I knew they were in good hands onboard the ship still, but that didn't stop me missing them.

I rolled out of bed, found my slippers and a robe, and went in search of coffee.

Drifting off to sleep the previous evening, I came up with a way to find out more about the money. It was plausible someone in the church council would know something, but I had another idea I believed stood a better chance of hitting pay dirt and would avoid needing Barbie to employ her assets. Allen Gibson and the vicar himself were the two people most familiar with the church finances and neither was available to answer my questions.

However, I was sure the police would have taken the ledgers from Allen's house when they removed his body and opened the investigation. They would have looked into the church bank accounts from a forensic perspective, so if I wanted to know more about the missing money, it was to them I needed to turn.

You, of course, are thinking Chief Inspector Quinn wasn't going to tell me anything and you would be right. I wasn't going to ask him though. I knew other officers in the local constabulary, ones who might be more forthcoming.

I didn't have numbers for anyone though unless you count nine, nine, nine, but I had a solution for that too.

Jermaine was in the kitchen when I arrived, the smell of coffee dragging me through the house like one of the Bisto Kids.

"Good morning, madam."

I bade him the same and slid into a seat at the kitchen table where the day's paper was set out waiting for me next to a glass of freshly squeezed orange juice.

"Where's Barbie?" I enquired, my attention on the front page of the paper.

"I believe she is in the gym, madam."

Of course she was. The news made me glad to have been left in bed this morning. Barbie saw to my exercise program and wasn't so sadistic that she thought I needed to do something every day.

Upon my request, Jermaine produced a ham and mushroom omelette. Part of me still hankered after a fat bacon sandwich loaded with HP sauce, but I had learned what gave me energy and what made me feel sluggish and tried my hardest to think of food as a fuel source, instead of the most glorious treat I could give myself multiple times a day.

My plate empty, I sent a message to Albert.

'I think we should concentrate on finding out what the money was for. I am heading into Rochester. Do you want to see if anyone on the church council knows more about it?'

Albert's reply came through in less than a minute.

'I was going to suggest much the same thing. Felicity suggested we team up, so I'll take her with me. She and I can cover the village in half the time if we work together. Sound good?'

'*Yes,*" I texted back. '*Stay in touch. Let me know if you get anywhere.*'

It seemed that we were set. There was a course of action for each of us to follow and Albert was right that we would get more done coming at the problem separately.

"Your plans for the day, madam?" Jermaine enquired, pausing for a moment to hear my reply when he collected my breakfast plate.

Feeling cryptic, I wiggled my eyebrows at him. "We're heading into Rochester, sweetie. Pick whichever car you feel like using today."

Tree Rats and Irritating Husbands

Rex sampled the air. There were squirrels around. In his garden earlier this morning when his human let him out to mark the fence, he consulted Dmitry and Angus, his Great Dane and West Highland terrier neighbours.

They reported the same thing he was seeing: the squirrels were more organised than usual and significantly more brazen.

It would not do. It would not do at all.

"Come along, Rex," Albert called to get his dog's attention. The giant German Shepherd was staring up at the oak tree in their garden again.

Albert knew his dog had a thing with squirrels. It was like they were his mortal enemy or something. It was the same thing with seagulls, though the birds tended to give Rex a wide berth these days for some reason Albert could not understand.

Rex let his eyes linger on the branches above for a few more seconds, staring with malice in the general direction of whatever fluffy-tailed nightmares there might be looking back down at him from their hidden vantage points.

"Rex!" Albert called again, becoming impatient.

He locked the back door and walked to the side gate; there was no reason to walk back through the house to go out the front.

Rex trotted to catch up, the sound of squirrels running down the tree trunk to get to his garden proving almost enough to send him back the way he came.

"*They're only doing it to wind you up*," Rex told himself. He knew it was true, but a reckoning had to come soon either way.

In the street, Albert had to choose which direction to go. Or would have if his neighbour opposite hadn't spotted him.

"Albert, old boy!" called Wing Commander Roy Hope, waving his walking cane in the air to make himself more visible as he came out of his house.

Seeing Roy reminded Albert that both he and his wife were members of the church council. Albert waited for Roy to reach him.

"Money," Albert introduced the topic.

Roy hiked one eyebrow.

"It appears to be at the centre of this mystery with the vicar. What can you tell me about the church roof fund?"

"The roof fund?" Roy repeated. "Not a lot, old boy. I know the roof has a few leaks and some cracked tiles. To be expected though, it's hundreds of years old. There are charity drives year round to collect money for various causes, the roof is just one of them. I don't think the repairs are imminent, but whether that's because they haven't got enough money yet or because it simply isn't bad enough to worry about, I cannot say. Is the roof important?"

"The roof? No, I don't think so, but the missing money is. We want to know when it went missing and how much money we are talking about. Who among the members of the church council might know?"

"Oh, um … I might need to consult the oracle on that one, old boy."

Albert knew without having to ask that Roy was talking about his wife.

They were just turning toward Roy's front door when a car cruised along the street to park outside Albert's house. A polite beep of the horn drew their attention and Albert waved at Felicity.

Rex could smell Buster the moment the car door opened, Mindy stopping the overly enthusiastic bulldog from leaping into the road by looping an arm around his entire body.

"Calm down, dog," she coached, carefully plopping him down but keeping two fingers hooked through his collar.

"*Rex!*" Buster barked, his stubby tail wagging. "*We're here to help solve a murder and we got to leave the cat at home! Isn't that wonderful?*"

Rex agreed wholeheartedly. "*Yay! No cats. We do have a squirrel issue though.*"

Buster stopped moving, his whole body freezing to pay complete attention.

"*Fluffy tree rats? Just point the way and Devil Dog will lead the charge.*"

"*Good. I like your attitude, but this is going to take strategy, not just enthusiasm. Here's what I have planned …*"

While the dogs talked, above them the humans did likewise.

"Morning, ladies," hallooed Roy, waving his walking cane in greeting. "Albert wants to get around the village to see the church council members. Hopefully, one of them knows something about the money missing from the church roof fund."

The door to his house opened, Beverly appearing in the doorway. Her feet still bore house slippers and without a coat, she wrapped her arms around her body when she ventured a few steps outside. Closing the door to keep the cold from getting in, she frowned at her husband.

"Are you planning to go gallivanting again? You know you always get into trouble when you go anywhere with Albert."

"Beverly, my queen," Roy cooed, "whatever can you mean? Admittedly, the old boy and I have gotten into a few scrapes, but nothing that should worry your pretty little head."

Beverly's frown deepened. "You got shot, Wing Commander Hope. Or had you forgotten that little injury?"

"You got shot?" Mindy looked for someone to confirm, her face shocked.

Roy wiggled his eyebrows at her. "'Twas nothing, my dear. The bounder wasn't fast enough to do more than wing me."

"Wing you," repeated Beverly, her eyes rolling. "I'll do more than wing you. Now stop flirting with girls a quarter your age, you old reprobate, and make sure you are wrapped up warm. I don't have the time or the energy to tend to you when you have a cold."

"You're not coming with us?" asked Albert.

"I have plans for today."

Roy whispered from one side of his mouth, the words muffled by his bushy grey/white moustache, "She's getting her hair coloured and cut. She went grey thirty years ago and has been in denial ever since."

"What was that?" growled Beverly, a threatening tilt now present on her brow.

Roy offered her pure innocence. "Nothing, my love. Merely clearing my throat."

Beverly glared for a further few seconds before relaxing her features to look at Albert.

"I have other plans," she repeated. "I don't want the two of you causing strife though." Aiming her eyes at Felicity, she said, "I shall assume the four of you are planning to split up so you can cover more ground." It was more of an order than a question.

Taken a little aback and feeling like she was in the middle of a minor domestic, Felicity said, "Um, I guess that makes sense."

Beverly seized her chance. "Jolly good. Please take my husband with you. I'm sure the dogs will be happier together anyway so Albert can accompany Mindy. All agreed?"

Again, her question was nothing of the sort and her eyes were boring into Roy's, daring him to counter her instructions or attempt to whisper something to his co-conspirator standing two feet to his right.

"Sounds like a capital idea," Roy cheered, clapping his hands together to get everyone moving.

Albert smiled and shook his head. His relationship with Petunia had been quite different, but then he was a far less gregarious character than Roy and could not recall ever having gone out of his way to annoy his wife – something Roy specialised in doing.

"Oh, one thing, Beverly," Albert remembered he had a question for her. "Who among the church council is most likely to know the details of the church roof fund?"

Blue Moon

I checked with Barbie to confirm she would hang out with Hideki for a while. They were both young and in love and spending far too little time together in my opinion. He needed to study, but had been hard at the books since we arrived at my house several days ago.

He could take a break so they could do something as a couple. We would be back on the ship soon enough and into a working routine. If they didn't get out now they would miss the chance and who knew when we would be back in England again.

Barbie protested a little, insisting she should help with the investigation, but her heart wasn't in it.

Setting off in the Aston Martin, the one car in my collection that didn't come from the Maharaja, we headed across the county to get to Rochester.

I was behind the wheel for once – it's *my* car – and thoroughly enjoying the power under my right foot. The distance is perhaps fifteen miles from point to point, and through countryside the whole way if one chooses not to take the most direct route.

I parked behind my old office, selecting one of the two spaces assigned to it. Noting with disappointment that the other space was empty, I nevertheless checked the door to see if Mike Atwell was there.

I had lunch with him just two days ago, but it would have been nice to drop by to see my old office. No such luck because he wasn't there, and I felt the vicar's case was too pressing to delay looking for him.

Instead, I accessed Rochester's cobbled High Street via a gap in the wall and turned right. Just a few yards further along the street I came to the office of another P.I. firm: Blue Moon Investigations.

The owner, Tempest Michaels, and I have become friends, working together more than once when our cases have aligned. Most recently he came to my rescue in Hampshire at the climax of the San José treasure hunt. To be fair, it wasn't so much Tempest as it was his hired muscle Big Ben who came to the rescue, and it wasn't me he was rescuing, but Barbie, with whom he is quite openly in love.

That was less than a week ago, and here I was again about to ask him for help. Sort of, anyway.

Marjory the receptionist looked up when the door opened. She recognised me instantly, rising from her chair to greet me. A lady in her late middle age, she is roughly the same height as me. Her ash-blonde hair showed just the faintest trace of the roots coming through, and she was dressed for the day in thick woollens to ward against the cold breeze that had to sneak in each time someone opened the office door.

"Is Amanda here?" I enquired of her once we had hugged.

Her eyebrows demonstrated her surprise; she'd expected me to want Tempest.

"She is. One moment," Marjory turned her head to the side so she wasn't bellowing in my face. "Amanda!"

She had a voice that would rival a foghorn.

I heard Amanda mutter something that might have been, "I'll call you back," followed by the sound of a phone being returned to its cradle.

Three seconds later she appeared in the door to her office at the back of the building.

"Patricia?" she looked surprised to see me.

Tempest's voice echoed out from the office next to Amanda's. "Patricia?"

He came out of his office with a client, a big man somewhere between Tempest and Big Ben in terms of stature, height, and muscle.

Tempest jogged to catch up to his partner/girlfriend, the client following for some reason.

Both Tempest and Amanda shook my hand and then Jermaine's. Then Tempest angled his body to one side, making space for his client to get through.

"Patricia, this is Darius Kane."

The man extended his hand, and I took it, curious to learn why I was meeting him.

"I've heard a lot about you," Darius said in an Australian accent. "Read a lot too for that matter. Tempest told me he knew you, but I thought he was just blowing smoke."

"I have no need to do so," Tempest remarked. Looking my way, he explained, "Darius is an old army buddy. We met when Darius took an exchange posting and spent two years with the British Army. It turned out to be when Iraq kicked off again, so we got to eat the same sand for a while."

"And bleed into it," added Darius, his throw away remark clearly reflecting the truth of it.

"Darius came to see me about opening his own branch of Blue Moon back where he lives on the Gold Coast of Australia."

"Oh," I looked at the rugged Australian with a more appraising eye.

He chuckled, a deep laugh that emanated from inside his chest.

"Yes, it's something of a change from soldiering, but Tempest assures me all I need is a logical approach, a cool head, and the willingness to smack criminals around when it comes to it."

I thought about that for a moment before saying, "I guess that about sums it up." Not that it described my business, but Blue Moon tackled a whole different subculture of lowlifes to the ones I usually meet.

Darius angled to go around the group, talking as he headed for the door.

"Nice meeting you, Patricia," he said, "I only got in a few hours ago and I need to grab some tucker before I starve to death. Some sleep wouldn't hurt either. I shall hope to see you again while I'm here."

"Are you staying long?" I asked before he could get to the door.

"A week. Just to shadow Tempest and learn what I can from the master."

Amanda let a smile tease her face, but said nothing.

Defending himself, Tempest raised his hands, "I never claimed to be a master of anything."

Darius grabbed the door, hanging in the doorway when he said, "Regardless, I'll be here for a while getting my head around the work before I head back to start my own franchise. Tempest has stumped up all the start-up money." With that he was gone, his silhouette vanishing into the crowd behind the frosted glass windows.

With the office suddenly quiet, Amanda turned her attention back to the reason for my visit.

"Everything okay?" she asked.

"Is this a social or business visit?" Tempest enquired, angling his body toward the visitors' seating area where I knew he served really good coffee from a very expensive machine.

Stopping by for one of his brews was enough reason to come in, but encouraging him to get busy with the unctuous, dark liquid, I got to the point of my visit.

"I need to make contact with Patience." I was looking firmly at Amanda when I said it.

The request caused a small jolt; it was not what Amanda expected to hear. She recovered immediately though, reaching for her back pocket to retrieve her phone.

"I can arrange that easily enough. Do you want her number to call her yourself, or shall I call her now?"

Jermaine accepted a white porcelain cup of steaming black Columbian coffee from Tempest, setting it on the table to my front before taking another for himself.

"Please call her, Amanda. It's to do with an ongoing case. I met her at the scene though I cannot speculate if she is still involved. I'm hoping she will be able to answer a couple of questions about the evidence collected."

Amanda made no comment; we both knew Patience wasn't allowed to discuss ongoing investigations in detail and also that she happily bent the rules whenever it suited her.

Amanda hit the green button to connect the call and the speaker button so we could all hear the conversation. Setting her phone in the centre of the low coffee table, she took a cup of coffee from Tempest and blew on the surface while we all waited for the call to connect.

"Yo, Blondie! Wassap?" Patience is very colloquial.

"Good morning, Patience," Amanda replied in a measured, calm manner. "I have Patricia Fisher at the office with me. Are you in the area?"

"Patricia is there? Sure, I'm in the car with Brad. I can be there in ten minutes."

Amanda said, "Hi, Brad." I guess she knew the call was going out over the speaker in the squad car.

Brad said, "Help," in a terrified tone.

It caused a pause at our end, the four of us exchanging looks before a grin pulled at Amanda's mouth.

"She got the keys first, didn't she?"

Brad wailed, "She tricked me. Sent me to grab drinks and hooked the keys when I wasn't looking."

The questioning look on my face caused a snigger from Amanda and she hissed, "Patience is a terrible driver. It's like being on a roller coaster with no restraints."

"Hey, I heard that," Patience snapped.

Amanda laughed openly. "So slow down. We'll see you in five minutes."

"I said ten."

"Yes, but you're probably doing twice the speed limit."

"Of course I am. They gave me a car with flashing lights and a siren. What else are they for if not to get places fast?"

Amanda ended the call, and we chatted about the San José treasure, a case Tempest and Big Ben found themselves drawn into.

"Hey, where is the big fella, anyway?" asked Barbie.

"Injured," smirked Amanda, her grin demanding she expand which she did by pointing between her legs. "Got a little too amorous with some ladies and needed a few stitches somewhere he would rather not have them."

Jermaine tried hard not to wince at the suggested nature of Big Ben's injury.

From the reception desk, Marjory tutted. "*Some ladies*. Serves him right. The way that boy carries on with women. It shouldn't be allowed."

Tempest didn't exactly leap to his friend's defence, but he did say, "I can assure you all parties are consenting."

Marjory continued to mutter her thoughts, and I used the break in conversation to turn the subject away from me and what I am doing.

"What are you guys working on at the moment?" I aimed the question at both Tempest and Amanda. Anything interesting to keep you all busy?"

"And where is Jane?" asked Barbie, enquiring after the third member of the detective team.

Tempest fielded. "Well, Jane is currently investigating a private case, by which I mean something without a client."

"She's working with a police detective at Buckingham Palace," explained Amanda. "It started months ago with a case involving a dragon."

I checked with Jermaine and Barbie, both of whom looked just as mystified as I felt.

"I didn't read anything about that in the papers," I pointed out, realising my foolishness the moment the words left my mouth. "Of course I didn't."

Around a nod of acknowledgement, Tempest said quietly, "It's not the kind of news the palace would ever want to admit. Anyway, with all the recent royal deaths, there are persons who believe there is someone behind it all."

"And that is what Jane is investigating?"

"As well as other cases. Cassie, the detective she is working with at the palace, asked for her help. It would appear she is getting all too little of it from her bosses."

"Goodness." I wasn't sure what else to say, and the room fell quiet in a contemplative way for a moment. Circling back to my original question, I nudged Tempest to talk about what he was up to.

"There must be something weird and fantastic on your books."

He downed his coffee, setting his delicate, white porcelain cup on the table before speaking.

"We have someone re-enacting Grimm fairy tales," he reported, somehow making the statement sound completely normal.

Barbie blinked a couple of times. "What, like Red Riding Hood?"

Tempest met her eyes. "Exactly like that."

"And there is a demon," Amanda revealed.

Jermaine crossed himself.

"Don't worry, it's not real," Tempest assured us. "A few miles from here, out in the middle of pretty much nowhere, a couple came across a seven-foot-tall figure with antlers and cloven hoofs. It was standing in the middle of the road and their attempts to avoid it crashed their car and put them both in hospital. They are my clients."

"Any leads?" I enquired, killing time until Patience arrived.

Tempest leaned back into his chair, drawing one leg up to cross it over the other knee.

"I think we have it all figured out, actually. We caught a lucky break with their son. They told us he had a tattoo of the same demon thing on his arm, and it turns out he was coerced into getting it. That led to the poor guy being drawn into a criminal ring. The demon will be nothing of the sort and we are hoping to find out more tonight."

Amanda gave a small shake of her head and rolled her eyes. "Tempest is planning to break into the tattoo parlour. By himself," she added, clearly disapproving.

Tempest huffed out a breath. "We have been over this, darling. The risk is low, and I am taking Darius with me."

"And what if the tattoo parlour is the base for the gang of drug dealers and thugs? What then? You need to wait for Big Ben to be back to fighting strength."

I was beginning to feel like I was in the middle of a domestic, but there was something else that made me interrupt – a sense of duty.

"Can we assist?" I volunteered. When Tempest and Amanda looked my way, I said, "We," I made sure to include Barbie and Jermaine, "Owe you many times over. I, for one, would feel much better if you would allow us to accompany you tonight."

Barbie echoed my thoughts, saying, "If there are people to thump, Jermaine is very good at it, and I bet Hideki will want to come too. He's like a modern-day Bruce Lee."

I could see Tempest was going to argue and I shot him down before he could. Even though I had a case to investigate, I was going along with him tonight. He gave up trying to talk me out of it when he saw the steel in my expression.

Relenting, Tempest steered the conversation back to the reason for my visit.

"Any clue who might be behind it if not the vicar?" asked Tempest.

I wasn't sure how to answer other than to give the honest response of, "Not one clue. Yet." It was bugging me that so far, with Albert's help thrown in, we had nothing remotely resembling a lead and every stone we looked under made the vicar look more guilty.

Patience arrived six minutes after Amanda hung up, twirling the keys to the squad car from one index finger and looking like she was having the best day.

"Hey, everyone, how's it going? Got any of that fantastic coffee?"

Tempest poured her a cup and a second for Brad who wasn't as shaken or as scared as he might want to let us believe.

We shook hands and caught up for a moment, but Patience proved how astute she is by guessing the reason for my visit.

"You have questions about your vicar?"

"About the missing money," I replied. "I know it looks like he is guilty ..."

"He's still denying any involvement in the two murders so far as I know," Patience supplied.

"Has he said anything about the money? What it was for? How much we are talking about?"

"Well, I can tell you the numbers. I know that much because I heard Quinn telling his boss. The vicar embezzled twenty-five thousand pounds from the roof fund almost five years ago."

"Twenty-five thousand?" I was surprised to hear it was such a small amount. I mean, not that most people have that kind of money just lying around, but it was hardly worth killing for.

"Yup, that's all. But," she made a big thing of the *but*, "he took a further ten thousand just a few days ago."

"So thirty-five in total." It still didn't sound like enough to kill for though I suppose some might disagree. It is more than many would earn in a year.

"Here's the weird thing though; he was paying it back."

Everyone pulled the same confused face.

"Paying it back?" repeated Tempest. "Recently? In lumps?"

I jumped in with a question of my own. "How much of the original amount had he returned to the roof fund?"

Patience looked me dead in the eye. "About half."

What did that mean? The vicar was embezzling money, but treating the roof fund like an interest-free loan. Five years ago, just a few months after he arrived in East Malling, he took twenty-five thousand pounds, then started repaying it only to take a further ten thousand pounds recently.

Is that what caused the row the vicar's wife overheard? That was just a few days ago, so the timing was about right. Allen had a full-time job, so he probably didn't check the church bank account more than once or twice a month. He'd spotted the hefty withdrawal and reacted as anyone would, confronting the vicar for an explanation.

Yet again, I was solving the case in my head, but finding the vicar guilty. Allen accused the man who took the money, possibly threatening to expose the truth if it wasn't returned and Reverend David killed him to cover up his secret.

His dangerous secret.

Confusing Silhouettes

R ex and Buster led the way, their noses aimed at the street ahead.

"Any idea where we are going?" Buster asked.

Rex sniffed the air, testing it for squirrels before saying, *"Something to do with the church and money. I stopped listening after that."*

Buster frowned. *"But we're going the wrong way to get to the church."*

"That we are. That's not the confusing thing though."

"It isn't?"

"No. What I find confusing is the need to investigate at all." Now that Buster was listening, Rex explained all that had happened in the last couple of days. *"I chased a man from a house. Someone had been killed in the house and I know it was murder because I heard the humans talking about it. Also, the house stank of police officers."*

"They have a particular smell?"

"They do, actually. A blend of the polish and beeswax they use on their boots, the starch on their uniform. The cotton used on their uniforms even has a smell if one's nose is correctly attuned to detect it."

"Well, your nose is better than mine."

"Perhaps," Rex conceded, knowing it was many times more powerful than his flat-faced friend. *"But my time as a police dog is what allows me to know the police were in the house. The point is, I chased a man from the house, and he was in there when he ought not to have been."*

"So you think he is the killer."

"I do." Rex confirmed. *"Not just because of that, but because my human led me to his house the next day where the police were arresting him. I saw his mate; they were arguing about money."*

"Isn't it shocking how often humans do that?" Buster remarked.

"I find it no stranger than when they walk past perfectly good food in the street to go and buy other food from a shop and then complain about money."

"Yup. What's with that?"

Buster and Rex could have exchanged anecdotes about their humans and complained about human behaviour in general for hours, but they felt the tension in their leads as both were encouraged to stop.

Mindy stopped short of the gate.

"You first, Albert," she insisted. "I'm not the sleuth here. I'm the plucky sidekick."

Albert went ahead, saying, "Yes, I saw you in action last night. 'Kick' is the right word."

They were at Gwen Phelps' house on Easterbridge Lane. Beverly hadn't been able to give them a name she thought most likely to know about the details of the roof fund, so they were going door to door to speak with as many of them as possible. Most were retired persons, though there were a few members of the church council still young enough to be holding down jobs.

Albert expected them to be at home during the day and was rewarded for his hopeful efforts when the front door opened to reveal Gwen drying her hands on an apron.

"Albert?" she questioned. "Sorry, I was just washing up the breakfast things. Do you want to come inside?"

It was rather cold to be standing around outside if there was an option to go in and he felt certain Gwen had no desire to wash the warmth from her property by keeping the front door open.

He took a moment to introduce Mindy since he was certain Gwen wouldn't know her.

"Oh, I figured she must be one of your grandchildren. Well, come in, come in, the pair of you, please."

With the door closed, the dogs were instructed to stay next to the welcome mat while the humans traipsed through to the kitchen.

"Is this to do with the vicar?" Gwen asked, stripping off the apron to hang it on a hook behind the kitchen door.

"Yes, Gwen. Specifically I have questions about the church's roof fund. Were you aware there was a large sum missing from it?"

Albert knew to watch the interviewee to see how she reacted, but there was no faking the surprise she showed at his news.

"Missing! How much?"

"Twenty-five thousand that was taken almost five years ago," Albert recited the information Patricia sent him not two minutes before they knocked on Gwen's door. "Plus another ten thousand this month." He chose to omit that the vicar had been returning it as it wasn't relevant to his questions.

"Thirty-five thousand? But that's got to be almost everything we've managed to cobble together over more than a decade of hard charity work. Who took it?"

Albert met Gwen's eyes, waiting for the penny to drop.

When it did, she gasped. "The vicar?" She used the kitchen counter for support in moving to a chair set at her small kitchen table. Lowering herself into it, she appeared lost for words until she said, "So he's guilty then. The vicar killed Allen and then he killed poor old Beryl." She snapped her eyes up to look at Albert again. "Allen was going to expose him, and he had to kill Beryl because she saw him leaving the house."

"Beryl said she saw a woman."

Gwen snorted a laugh. "Have you seen the vicar?"

Albert didn't answer the obviously rhetorical question. Instead he waited for Gwen to expand.

"He's not exactly the biggest fellow. Half the women are the same height or taller and he has a blonde ponytail." Gwen made her points in a mocking tone, watching Albert's face to see when his brain caught up.

Albert's eyes flared in realisation. Gwen was right. Why hadn't he seen it before? Beryl could so easily have seen the vicar in the dark on the opposite side of the street and thought it was a woman.

Continuing to mock her guest, though not cruelly, Gwen added, "You're investigating because the vicar asked you to find the person behind Allen's murder? Surely that was nothing more than a clever or half-panicked ruse to throw everyone off the scent."

"Perhaps," Albert conceded. Truthfully, his faith that the vicar had to be innocent was waning. Like Patricia, he came into the investigation fully believing there was something Chief Inspector Quinn was missing, but the vicar didn't seem to be doing anything to help his cause and clearly had no alibi for the murders or he would have already been released.

He wasn't ready to throw in the towel just yet, but so far every question Albert asked took him another step in the wrong direction.

Changing tack, Albert came at the subject of the vicar from another angle.

"Gwen have you ever seen or heard the vicar arguing with Allen?"

"Before he stabbed him in the back, you mean?"

Albert winced. "I'm still hoping that is not the case, Gwen, but did you?"

Gwen pursed her lips, puffing out her cheeks while she thought.

"No, I suppose I don't recall any cross words. In fact, I always thought they were friends. I believe they went golfing together a few times."

Albert made a mental note. They might have been friends, but that wouldn't have stopped the relationship going sour if Allen discovered the vicar was taking more money.

More money.

Something had to have changed recently.

The vicar took a large chunk of money, Albert was willing to take that as, ahem, gospel now. It happened five years ago and whatever the reason, the church treasurer had to know about it. Perhaps Allen Gibson himself set up the repayment plan and then kept the matter secret to avoid the embarrassment that would surface if the missing money became public knowledge.

That all changed when the vicar took another ten thousand. Patricia already confirmed it was the vicar who withdrew it.

Interrupting his thoughts, Gwen asked, "Would you like a cup of tea? Or coffee? I have both. I have some biscuits too. The good ones with all the chocolate on."

Albert declined as politely as he could. He had much to ponder and there were other church council members with whom he needed to speak.

Concrete Evidence

"**A**re you sure you want to do this, madam?"

Standing outside Maidstone Police Station for the second time in two days, I gritted my teeth. Jermaine's question framed the very reason I was still outside in the cold air and not inside getting on with it.

"No," I replied with a sigh. "I genuinely don't want to do this. Speaking with Chief Inspector Quinn is like giving birth: it's painful, it takes too long, and all too often it is where the real trouble starts."

Jermaine accepted my response without comment and turned to head back to the car, only reversing direction when I started forward.

"That doesn't mean I'm not going to do it. Millions of women put themselves through the experience every year. Why should I be spared?"

I yanked the outer door open with more energy than I felt and stormed across to the reception desk before I could change my mind or chicken out.

"Mrs Fisher?" It was the same duty sergeant as the other day, though the constable with him was now a young woman with dark hair pinned up into a bun. "Back again so soon?"

The constable stared at me for a few seconds, confirming for herself that I was who she thought before becoming suddenly conscious of what she was doing and looking away.

"Yes. I need to speak to Chief Inspector Quinn," I announced, getting the words out quickly. "Is he in?"

The sergeant reached to pick up a phone from its cradle on his desk. "I will check, but I believe he is. I will need to tell him what your request pertains to, Mrs Fisher."

I opened my mouth to answer, but closed it again without speaking. What did I want to say? This was hardly the first time I'd confronted the chief inspector. However, always in the past I had the answers and was coming to present them so I could ruin his day. That was not the case on this occasion. I needed information only he or the vicar could supply.

"Please tell him that Patricia Fisher wishes to discuss the recent double homicide in East Malling."

I got a nod of acknowledgement, the sergeant pressing a button and holding the phone to his ear. A heartbeat later he started talking.

Less than a minute later, the door leading from reception into the station proper swung open to reveal a man I truly loathe. Oh, there are other men I have learned to dislike or even hate, but they were almost all criminals of one kind or another. Somehow Quinn was on the right side of the law and still managed to harbour in me feelings of intense mistrust and dislike.

He stood in the doorway, staring at me with a haughty expression. He didn't say anything, his petty need for one-upmanship dictating he wait for me to speak first.

I had no time for his nonsense, so I strode forward, crossing the distance with my hand extended. He could take it and be civil, or he could snub me in public and in full view of his subordinates. That would get their tongues wagging.

Quinn is wiser than that though, so he took my hand and acted as if we were old friends.

"Patricia, so lovely of you to stop by. Won't you please follow me?"

Jermaine started forward too, but Quinn held out a hand to stop him.

"Just Mrs Fisher, I'm afraid. My office is rather small – government budgets and all that." He made it sound like an apology, but he knew what he was doing. By separating me from my bodyguard he hoped to somehow weaken me. Or weaken my resolve perhaps.

Tailing him through the open plan police station I smiled to myself: his tactic was having the opposite effect.

He held his office door for me, clearly intending to close it once I was inside.

I thanked him, remaining polite, and took a seat opposite his desk. Looking around I noted how he was being honest about the size of it; there was barely room for one more person to join us. It was sparsely decorated with few personal adornments on the walls, shelves, or his desk.

To one side, an eight by twelve inch photograph showed a younger Ian Quinn still wearing the rank of constable. He was joined by three men in uniform all of an age that suggested they were the generation above. They looked too alike to be anything other than brothers so one of them had to be his father. A fifth man, a generation older again, wore civilian clothing, but the medals pinned to the breast pocket of his jacket let the world know he had been a police officer too, though undoubtedly in an age when they were police*men*. He had to be the patriarch and I questioned if the old man in the picture was the first in the family or if the tradition went back more generations.

The Quinn boys, law enforcers to the core. Why bother recruiting them when new officers could just be bred.

Tracking my eyes, Quinn settled onto one corner of his desk, a position that guaranteed I would have to crane my neck to look up at him. He was all about the powerplays, but it simply told me he was nervous – a confident person would feel no need to resort to such pathetic tactics.

"My father, grandfather, and uncles," he explained.

I believed he was about to launch into a long-winded spiel about his family, so I cut him off with a question.

"What did the vicar need the money for?" I was abrupt in my delivery and speared his eyes with mine, determined to hold his gaze until he gave me an answer.

"He refuses to say."

I guess he told me because it did me no good.

Quinn skewed his lips to one side for a moment, eyeing me contemplatively before continuing.

"Mrs Fisher, we are not enemies."

"I agree."

He held up a hand to stop me from saying anything more.

"Are you sure? I ask because I feel you view me as precisely that. I am the only law enforcement officer in this room." He could see I was about to speak my mind and pushed on rudely to stop me from doing so. "However, let me make it clear that I recognise your ability as a detective, an investigator."

Okay, so he was disarming my ire before it could get up to speed and I allowed him to continue talking without interruption.

"This latest case, in which we are both invested, serves as a prime example. Reverend David Gentry embezzled a large amount of money rather than take a loan. This, in itself, is not a matter for the police. The church would need to sort this out. However, the two murders appear to be directly linked to the embezzled money. He refuses to divulge what the money was used for, and our forensic accountants are yet to find where it went. Most likely this is because he withdrew cash and used it to pay for something. Or perhaps gambled it away. Whichever the case, I believe he had been able to work out a repayment plan with the treasurer and was quietly putting back the money he took."

This aligned with what I believed.

"However, the vicar took a further large sum earlier this week and it proved to be the catalyst for his murderous rampage. He killed Allen Gibson to hide his crime and felt forced to kill Beryl Forrester when she revealed having seen him leave Allen's property on the night of his murder."

I felt obliged to argue.

"According to the witnesses who heard her testimony, Beryl saw a woman, not the reverend."

Quinn offered me a sympathetic smile.

"Come now, Mrs Fisher. The Father is short for a man and slight too. Combine those characteristics with his long hair when seen at night across the road by a woman knocking on the door of her one hundredth birthday and I think we can assume she saw the vicar and not someone else."

"We can assume it. That is far removed from knowing we are right. Would you convict a man on such evidence?"

Quinn's eyes flared a touch.

"Yes. Indeed I would and the Crown Prosecution Service agree wholeheartedly. David Gentry cannot produce an alibi for the times when the murders took place. He refuses to divulge where the money went. His own wife stated that he had a fight with Allen Gibson days before he was killed and that the vicar chose to leave the house on the night of Allen Gibson's murder, returning some time later. Guess where he said he had been."

"Allen Gibson's house." I filled in the obvious blank.

"Precisely. To me that is as good as a confession."

"Except he hasn't confessed, has he." I pointed out.

"No. He states that Allen was alive when he left his house, but I'm afraid there is more, Mrs Fisher. We found the vicar's fingerprints on the jar of olive oil used to create the spill in Mrs Forrester's home. The one we were supposed to believe resulted in her broken neck. His fingerprints were on the knife found wedged in Allen Gibson's back, and the knife itself came from the vicar's kitchen."

He sat back on his desk, happily victorious.

"He is guilty, Mrs Fisher. As guilty as any killer I have ever met."

I exhaled slowly through my nose. The rush of new evidence against a man I believed to be innocent was a little overwhelming.

"I wish to see him," I requested, doing my best to make my voice sound indomitable.

A small snort escaped the chief inspector's nose.

"I'm afraid that won't be possible."

"Why not?"

"Because he is no longer here. I already told you the CPS approved my request that he be charged. They needed seconds to review the evidence. He was transported to His Majesty's Prison Maidstone two hours ago."

Family Ties

Miles from Patricia, but not too far from Albert and Mindy, Felicity and Roy were having about as much luck as everyone else.

"How many do you think we should visit?" Felicity asked. She was more involved than she had intended to be and really needed to be focused on the royal wedding arrangements. Her trip to the church yesterday had only been to see if there was anything to see – to hopefully alleviate her concerns and prove the vicar's arrest wasn't yet another dastardly tactic by whoever was behind all the ill fate her plans were seeing.

Far from thinking herself to be a sleuth, Felicity acknowledged her inability to see the links between the clues and struggled, for that matter, to even notice the clues were there.

Roy shrugged his shoulders. He wasn't a sleuth either. Give him a fighter plane and a mission and even at his age he was ready to do his part, but wheedling answers from suspects who might not wish to divulge the truth was not a skill he possessed.

"Having committed to help, I guess we keep going until someone makes a breakthrough and lets us know we can stop. Or we run out of people to visit."

They were leaving their fourth house and rather full of tea and cake/biscuits. Thus far they had stopped at Rose Tyler's place where she insisted they had to try her Battenburg cake. It was freshly made just yesterday and was a recipe she'd been perfecting for years.

From there they cut across two streets to stop in with Harry Dresden, a former verger, now retired from that role due to a tricky hip. His wife had a Victoria sponge they simply had to help her with. Martha Jones and Amy Pond went for biscuits rather than cake, and Felicity's ability to politely partake was wearing thin.

They were approaching the cottage belonging to Beatrix Crawford. She ran a small B&B at the outskirts of the village and had been part of the church council for at least five decades.

It took her a while to answer the door, no great surprise given that she was another member of the village in her nineties, but was pleased to see Roy when she pulled back the curtain to check who was there.

"Hello, Roy. Terrible weather we've been having recently."

"Rather chilly, yes," he agreed. "Do you know Felicity Philips?"

Beatrix allowed herself a moment to consult her memory before concluding, "No, I don't believe so. Have we ever met?"

"I'm a wedding planner," Felicity replied. "So our paths might have crossed if you've been to any weddings in the area in the last thirty years."

"Ooh, a few," Beatrix cackled. "I've got seven children, twenty-six grandchildren, fifty-four great grandchildren, and three great, great grandchildren. There have been a few weddings." Letting her smile drop, she added, "I don't recall ever seeing you though."

Needing the loo and certain there must be more than one inside Beatrix's B&B, Roy asked, "Do you mind if we come in? We're helping Patricia Fisher with an investigation – that terrible business with the vicar, and we need to ask a couple of questions."

Beatrix blinked and blinked again, processing the information and struggling to make sense of it.

"You have questions for me? You think I had something to do with the murders?"

"No, old girl. Nothing of the sort," Roy assured her. "The questions are about the church finances. We're hoping members of the council might be privy to information not publicly known."

Beatrix brought them inside, closing the door and pointing the way to the nearest downstairs toilet so Roy could deal with what was becoming a pressing matter.

Finding her in the living room a few minutes later, Roy took a seat on the couch next to Felicity. Beatrix looked comfortable in a wing-backed armchair facing the giant flatscreen TV in the corner, and had angled herself so she faced her guests.

Felicity hadn't waited for Roy; confident she could ask the questions they had without him.

"Beatrix doesn't know anything about the missing money, Roy," Felicity brought her companion up to speed." It had been the same story at every stop so far. They knew from Patricia that the vicar was responsible for the missing money, how much he had taken, when, and that he'd been slowly repaying it until earlier this week when he made another large withdrawal.

However, the church treasurer had kept it hidden from everyone and the vicar certainly never mentioned it.

"Have you asked about the vicar's relationship with Allen?"

Felicity nodded, but it was Beatrix who answered. "I've never known the vicar to fall out with anyone. Not like the last one. You remember him, Roy?"

Roy smirked knowingly. Reverend Geoffrey Grey had been an irascible old soul. Of course both Roy and Beatrix had been around long enough to recall when Angus was nicer to be around. When he arrived at the parish in the eighties, he had a family by his side, but the kids were already teenagers by then and within a few years had left home.

That ought to have heralded a new era where the married couple rekindle their relationship free from the burden of dependents in the house, yet his wife died just two years later, and both his general demeanour and the tone of his sermons turned sour.

Roy gave a small shake of his head. "I recall how receptive the community were to the new, young vicar and his wife when they arrived."

"Yes, very much so. Sadie brought so much energy with her too. I think that was a big part of it. The church is the hub of the community, and the community needs a vicar capable of pulling them all together."

Roy elected to keep quiet, thinking to himself that the pub made a perfectly good community hub and people went there to worship seven days a week.

"It's a surprise they've not started a family," Beatrix continued. "Especially given that she doesn't have one of her own."

Roy was about to agree and had opened his mouth to do so, when he stopped.

"No, hold on. That's not right." His eyes were up and right, consulting his memory to confirm what he knew about the vicar's wife. The archdeacon said the vicar moved so his new wife could be closer to her family. But now that he thought about it, he could not recall ever seeing her with parents or siblings attending one of her husband's services.

That failed to form conclusive proof, but was Beatrix correct?

Felicity had been waiting for Roy to form his next sentence, but his face had frozen and she was beginning to worry that he might be having a stroke. Only when he pursed his lips did she turn her face away from him to look at Beatrix again.

"I can assure you I am right," Beatrix argued, her remark meant for Roy, not Felicity, but seeing her male guest was still staring into space, she added, "The poor girl is an orphan."

The information conflicted with what the group told Felicity, so thinking with her best detective's head on – basically, trying to imagine what Patricia would do – she questioned what Beatrix believed.

"How do you know this, Beatrix?"

"She was in the foster system, love," Beatrix replied knowingly. "My Glenda, that's my youngest daughter, looked after her for two years right up until she turned eighteen. They cast them free at that point and they have to figure out how to fend for themselves. Oh, there's some support in place to make sure they don't starve to death or end up living on the streets but nowhere near enough in my opinion ..." Beatrix waffled on, speaking with knowledge, it seemed, about the national foster care crisis and what the government ought to be doing about it.

Roy's hand on Felicity's arm got her attention.

When she met his eyes, he said, "This changes things. We need to tell the others."

Beatrix was still talking, her subject now falling somewhere between which political party might do something to improve the system for orphaned or displaced children and the fact that all politicians should be imprisoned the moment they voice a desire to get into politics.

Roy and Felicity had to wait until she ran out of steam before announcing, "We need to go."

Fresh Plans

Albert felt rocked by the news. Had the archdeacon lied? Was she merely mistaken? Did Reverend David lie so the false story the archdeacon gave them was not of her creation?

He was at the park with Mindy where both dogs were enjoying some exercise. Roy and Felicity were on their way to rendezvous.

Weighing up his options, Albert chose to call Patricia.

She picked up almost the moment it started to ring.

"Albert, have you had any luck?"

"Well," he questioned whether he ought to label it as luck or not and settled for, "We have had something."

"Sounds ominous."

"Well, we set out to ask the church council members about the missing money, see if any of them knew more than the skimpy details we've already been able to learn. That got us squarely nowhere so far. However," he let the however hang like a foreshadowing, "we did learn something about the vicar's wife."

"Oh, do tell." Patricia was with Jermaine in a coffee shop in Maidstone. Her experience with Chief Inspector Quinn left her feeling out of sorts – she wasn't used to him getting the upper hand – so rather than delve straight back into the case, she suggested tea and cake.

Jermaine was never going to argue; he habitually did whatever his principal wanted, such was his chosen role.

The aptly named 'Rest-a-While' served doorstop-sized slices of cake and giant cookies a person could hide behind like a broadsheet newspaper. They also had a fine selection of teas from which she could pick, but there was little, to her mind, that could beat an Earl Grey.

"Well, she's an orphan," Albert began to explain. "That in itself is not important, I don't think. However, when we spoke to the archdeacon at Reverend David's previous parish, she claimed he left there so his wife could be closer to her family."

Patricia set down the delicate teacup she was holding.

"Do you believe the archdeacon lied?"

Albert sucked on his teeth before saying, "I wouldn't commit to that. I think it more likely she has a false memory or was fed a lie in the first place."

"But this goes back to the question of why the vicar left his parish to come to East Malling."

"That's right," Albert agreed. "There might be nothing to it ..."

Patricia felt a familiar itch at the back of her skull and chose to interrupt. "No, I think you may be onto something."

"Well, that would be a refreshing change. I'm waiting for Roy to return; it was he and Felicity who uncovered this little snippet. When he gets here, I think we'll organise ourselves and head back to Dover."

"Understood. Of course, the best person to ask might be the vicar's wife."

There was no way to argue Patricia's logic. "Are you going to tackle that side of things?"

Now on the spot, Patricia gave herself a second to mull it over. The poor woman wasn't having a good time of things and she'd already been questioned at length by the police and again when the local sleuths turned up unannounced on her doorstep. Was it fair to demand she answer more questions now?

Well, if she wanted her husband back, Patricia supposed it was a small price to pay. The evidence against him made the chances of clearing his name appear bleak, but she was not one to be so easily defeated. Her itchy skull told her there was still something off about the case and Patricia knew it would be hard to sleep until she knew what it was.

Nodding to herself, she reclaimed her teacup, pinky finger raised.

"Yes, Albert, I believe that I will. Good luck in Dover. Please let me know how things go."

Ending the call, she upended her cup, savouring the fine brew.

Back in East Malling Park, Albert tucked his phone away and called for his dog.

"Rex! It's time to go, Rex."

He squinted at the bushes on the far side of the field. The park was a safe place to take dogs since there was fence all the way around and only one way in or out. The field and woodland around its periphery funnelled toward the exit making it hard for dogs or even children to escape.

Large oak and sycamore trees dotted the field's expanse, giving shade where bushes grew and wildlife abounded.

Rising from the park bench on which she had chosen to recline, Mindy narrowed her eyes to spot Buster.

"Buster!"

"Rex!"

Neither dog appeared.

"Buster! Where the heck is he this time?"

Herding Squirrels

D mitry the Great Dane asked, *"Do you really think this will work?"*

Rex made the canine equivalent of a shrug. "You got a better idea?"

Angus, a West Highland terrier sniggered, *"Dmitry doesn't have any ideas full stop."*

Dmitry shot his eyes down at the scruffy white blob of a dog and considered lifting a back leg in his direction.

Rex's neighbours were far from the sharpest tools in the shed, but they were what he had to work with. Although, Rex mused, looking around at his assembled pack, he might be better off if it were just him and his neighbours.

He had Sheba, the border collie who was so highly strung she vibrated like a child mainlining caffeine. Next to her were Zig and Zag, a duo of Dalmatians. They were ageing and past their prime – hardly what he needed for this job, but still a significant improvement on Blaze, the Basset Hound. He was as good as blind his ears were so large. They hung over his face, but were more or less redundant because the loose skin of his forehead gathered where his eyebrows ought to be. Goodness knows where his eyebrows actually were, Rex pondered, probably somewhere close to his chin.

Barking to make the assorted dogs listen, Rex acted like a sergeant major on parade.

"You've got the plan and you each know your part in it. It really isn't all that difficult. The squirrels taunt us every chance they get, but they target us opportunistically, not in an organised way. That's what we can exploit."

Sheba twirled on the spot, barking each time her face passed Rex's.

"I'm ready! I'm ready! I'm ready! Just point me in the right direction. Let's get those fluffy suckers!"

"Sheba." Rex calmly tried to stop her from spinning. *"Sheba,"* he repeated.

Sheba spun again, her legs a black and white blur that was beginning to make Rex feel sick.

"SHEBA!" Rex barked abruptly, the sudden shock of it finally getting through the border collie's thick skull.

She stopped rotating, found time to say, *"What?"* before the dizziness caught up and she fell over.

Rex rolled his eyes.

"Look, folks, I honestly don't have the patience to go through it again. I'm going to my position. Either go to yours or don't. When Buster here ..." Buster all but saluted, puffing his chest out as he stood to attention, *"gives the signal, each of you will chase the squirrels on the ground toward the centre of the field. Got it?"*

Rex got a round of barks and yips in return.

"The squirrels will suddenly realise they are all running at each other from the various corners of the park and they will have no tree up which they can easily run."

"And that's when we murderise them," snarled Gomez, a tiny Chihuahua Rex couldn't see behind Dmitry's giant tree trunk of a leg and had managed to forget about.

"*No, Gomez, we do not murderise them,*" Rex sighed; this was the fourth time he'd had this particular discussion. "*We are domesticated dogs, not killers. Drop a dead squirrel at your human's feet and see how many gravy bones it gets you.*"

Gomez grumbled his thoughts on the matter at a barely audible volume.

"Rex!"

Rex jumped to his feet when his human's voice cut through the still midday air.

"*Time to go!*" he barked. "*Positions everyone. And wait for Buster's signal, okay?*"

Overexcited barks and yips filled the air, the small pack of dogs attempting to disburse in different directions at the same time which caused multiple collisions and pile ups.

Rex said, "*Whaaaa!*" when Gomez ran between his back legs, the tiny dog's tail tickling where Rex would rather not be tickled.

His heart thumping, for he still had nightmares about the vet removing parts he cherished, Rex watched to make sure everyone went where they were supposed to.

His human was coming closer, storming across the field, and shouting his name in an insistent manner. Buster's human was with him. It didn't look like the humans had been able to spot their hiding place yet, but the moment they broke cover the race would be on.

"*Now or never, Rex,*" he murmured to himself, trying to force a confidence he failed to feel. He was working with idiots. Easily distracted idiots for that matter, which are the worst kind.

Miraculously, the dogs all appeared to have gone to their appointed spots, each of them on the far side of one of the large trees dotted about the field. The dogs all experienced the same taunting each time they came to the park and got the same treatment all around the village and even in their own gardens. It happened so brazenly because the squirrels knew they could get away with it.

They would scurry down a tree, skitter into the open on the grass in full view of a dog and wait to be chased. Then, they would whip along the ground, the fuzzy little tails twitching only to reach the next tree and vanish up it.

The squirrel would disappear, but his friends and family were always waiting to pelt the dog with acorns or whatever else they could find, and the dog would be running full tilt to catch the fluffy menace and was thus unable to change trajectory to avoid the bombardment from above.

Today, the dogs were going to prove they were not to be trifled with.

Rex moved to his spot and looked to Buster who was positioned on a short mound like a baseball pitcher.

Looking around the field as if checking the bases, he checked once more with Rex before launching into a series of barks so filled with energy and gusto his front paws bounced off the ground.

Fifty yards away, Mindy and Albert stopped moving.

"What are they doing?" Mindy asked, her eyes wide as she tried to take in the scene playing out across the whole field.

Albert huffed and shrugged. "Damned if I know. That dog of mine is … you know what? I don't know what he is, but he always seems to be at the centre of something that defies explanation."

"Do we just get them?" Mindy wasn't sure such a thing was even possible. "Or wait for them to come to us?"

From a dozen points around the field, dogs were advancing in what could only be described as a choreographed pattern, the circle they formed tightening with each step.

They were out beyond the trees, but coming toward them. Albert and Mindy saw dalmatians, a chihuahua, a basset hound who kept stepping on his own ears and stumbling

... they were each trotting nonchalantly toward a tree so that every last tree in the centre section of the field was covered.

"What on Earth?" questioned Albert.

Squirrels descended from the trees, one or two at first, their twitching, hesitant movements pausing every yard or so to check their surroundings.

Rex saw the first squirrel reach the ground. It did so in full view of about half the pack and he held his breath watching to see which dog would break rank and dart forward. His money was on Gomez, the tiny chihuahua whose bloodlust ran deepest for some reason.

A second squirrel arrived on the ground more or less opposite the first. They didn't seem to see each other, their attention too closely focused on the dog they were choosing to taunt.

"*Just hold on,*" Rex begged, his own paws desperate to get moving. "*Just a few more seconds.*"

They didn't need every tree to yield a squirrel. Half of them would do. Enough to prove a point and send a message. Rex knew it could work. His experience with the seagulls in Arbroath showed him how a story could spread.

More squirrels reached the ground. It was happening just as he predicted.

"*DIE!*" snarled Sheba, the border collie unable to contain herself any longer. Her cry acted as a battle charge for all the other dogs, each bursting into a sprint to get to their next positions. Well, all except Blaze the basset hound whose best speed was more of an amble.

Rex dug his claws into the soft earth beneath his paws and leapt forward. Head down, he powered after the squirrel to his front. It was on the other side of the tree, but well aware of Rex and watching for him to start moving.

As Rex bolted forward, the squirrel did precisely as predicted – it turned left and ran for the next tree. Very specifically, it didn't try to get back up the tree it had just come down. That was the whole point.

The squirrels wanted the dogs to chase them; it was a game and they had been winning it for a long time.

Rex kept going straight, ignoring his base instinct that demanded he give chase. In the periphery of his vision he could see other dogs doing much the same, the flash of their fur registering deep inside his brain though he dared not take his eyes off the squirrels.

With its head start and ability to virtually fly across the ground, there was no hope Rex could ever catch his target, but that was where the genius of his plan took effect.

Approaching the base of the next tree, the squirrel got ready to leap.

And that was when the dog it hadn't seen stepped out from behind the trunk.

"Are you seeing this?" asked Albert. "That's not my imagination, is it?"

Mindy watched with rapt fascination. "Nope. I'm seeing it too."

Zag dropped his front paws and chest, his back end poised to leap. There was no way for the squirrel to get to the tree without being caught by the dog.

Panicked, it squealed, a sound that warmed Rex's heart.

Each squirrel had run directly toward the dog chasing the squirrel away from the next tree. Thus, each squirrel now found itself between trees with dogs on either side of it. Terrified, the zipping grey tree rodents did the only thing they could: they changed direction.

The dogs had successfully herded squirrels and they were belting into the centre of the field now, going faster than they had ever run before, and with no clear destination in mind.

Watching the ball of fluff perform what appeared to be a ninety-degree turn without having to even slow down, Rex had to dig his paws into the grass and lean hard. Zag was already giving chase, the spotty black and white dog racing to catch the squirrel.

Rex collided with him, but side on so their flanks smacked off each other. It did little to slow either dog and they took off again side by side.

Now facing into the circle, Rex could see the same thing happening all over the field. They were doing it! He could count six ... no, seven squirrels, all heading for the centre of the circle. Each had a pair of dogs hot on their heels and it was now that Rex spotted the one minor flaw in his plan.

Well, minor might be an underestimation.

The fleeing squirrels were being corralled into a tightening circle like a shoal of fish trapped inside a net. However, while the squirrels were hurtling towards one another, so were the dogs.

And none of them appeared to have noticed this rather inconvenient fact yet.

The dogs were staring intently at the twitchy, fluffy tail in front of their noses. Like the bright, glowing attraction that draws flying insects to their doom, the dogs could no more take their eyes off their targets than they could volunteer to become vegans.

Only Rex saw the impending danger and it was far too late for him to do anything about it.

His head up, Rex barked a warning and dug his paws into the grass. However, he was travelling altogether too fast to prevent taking part in the collision.

The other dogs saw it coming at the last second when their collective fields of vision filled with something other than squirrel butt.

The squirrels, having reached the centre point of the circle, leapt into the air, but not directly upward which would have guaranteed falling to earth to land on the pack of snarling canines. No, they found the gaps between the dogs, diving, elongating their bodies, and twisting in the air to avoid danger and death like *Neo* in the *Matrix*.

Likewise leaping to avoid injury, the dogs did anything they could to occupy a space that did not already have multiple dogs in it. Many simply closed their eyes and prayed to whichever deity they most strongly believed to be responsible for gravy bones and abandoned street kebabs.

Rex threw himself skyward, leaping over Gomez easily enough only to find Dmitry the Great Dane also airborne and coming right for him.

Rex whimpered, "*Ohhhhh, shiiiii ...*"

Across the field, Mindy winced, turning her head away from the carnage.

Albert shook his head and started walking. "I've said it before," he grumbled to himself. "But there is something unusual about that dog of mine."

Keeping pace with him, Mindy snorted a laugh. "You don't know the half of it. Buster thinks he's a superhero. Calls himself Devil Dog."

Albert stopped walking, his face full of question when Mindy turned to look at him. He recalled the first time he'd met the teenage woman at a wedding. He was on the run from the police at the time and therefore doing his best not to make acquaintances. However, Mindy's aunt, Felicity, also acted as though she knew what the dog was thinking.

Her cheeks flushing red, for she knew what she had done, Mindy tried to cover up her slip.

"I mean, that's what auntie calls him because he's always trying to do something heroic."

Albert looked less than convinced because he was, but chose to let it go.

The dogs were lying in a tangled pile of bodies, breathing hard and whimpering gently. Albert and Mindy were not the only owners on their way to collect their dogs and some were running, their pace dictating they would get there first.

Rex staggered to his paws, swaying a little. His skull hurt when it collided with Dmitry's and his neck felt compacted. When he landed, it was on top of several other dogs including Zag's sister Zig who did not appreciate the overly friendly closeness and was quick to slap him away for getting fresh.

Unable to keep up with the other dogs, Buster got to watch the entire debacle. Five seconds after the squirrels made it back to the trees and chittered their anger from branches far above the ground, Buster trotted up to Rex and sat to scratch his left ear with a back paw.

"*That was spectacular,*" he offered. "*Right up until the end when it went horribly wrong and all the squirrels got away.*"

Rex decided he would be best served by lying down again. Closing his eyes, he muttered, "*Yeah, tell me about it.*"

"*Oh, hey,*" said Buster. "*Your human is here.*" Wagging his stubby tail, Buster offered Mindy a goofy grin. "*We've been having fun with squirrels. Did you see?*"

Back to Dover

Mindy and Albert met Felicity and Roy at the edge of the field right next to East Malling train station. They could hear the announcer talking over the PA – the train to London Victoria was approaching.

"Is Rex all right?" asked Felicity.

Buster greeted her with a wagging tail and a dopey smile, but Rex had his head down, his tail was still, and he looked almost ... drunk.

Albert shrugged. "I think so." He dearly wanted to explain what he and Mindy saw, but doubted he could do it justice with words. Instead, he settled for, "He ran into another dog. I think he could probably do with a lie down."

"Oh dear," Felicity wasn't sure what else to say.

"We need to go back to Dover, old boy," Roy announced. "I don't think it requires all of us though and Felicity has other things she ought to be doing."

Mindy's eyebrows twitched. "Do you need me too, auntie?" She hoped not. Her job was okay, but trying to figure out who killed two people was far more fun.

Felicity shook her head. "Sorry, Mindy, I volunteered you to drive. I hope that's okay."

Relieved, Mindy smiled, "Sure. I can do that."

It was a tight squeeze getting three adults and two large dogs into her Mini, but they crammed in with Albert in the back, Rex draped across his lap and Roy riding shotgun with Buster between his legs. Albert had to sit with his legs at an angle so his knees had somewhere to go.

Thankful it was only a short trip, they left the village and glorious Kent countryside behind in favour of the motorway, arriving a little less than an hour later back in the suburb of Kingsdown.

They were back, but they lacked a start point.

One option was to find the archdeacon again. Albert could accuse her of lying, or adopt a more restrained approach to tease the truth from her, but he wondered if perhaps there might be a third choice – nose around the parish.

In his first visit, he noted the presence of a coffee shop operating out of the attached church hall. This was not uncommon, each church needing to do what it could to keep funds rolling in. The people working inside would all be volunteers, giving up their time to help their church, and they would only do so because they were invested members of that community.

Therefore they would know stuff.

Rex lifted his head, instantly regretted it, and laid it back on Albert's thigh with a small whimper and a sigh.

"Would you prefer to stay here, boy?" Albert asked, already planning to do just that regardless. It was possible the dogs would be allowed in, but unlikely and he hoped popping inside would not take too long.

"Cup of tea anyone?" he asked.

The Heart Strings

I drove home after tea in West Malling. I would have needed to pass it to get to the vicarage anyway, so I took the opportunity to stop. My shoes were hurting my feet and I wanted to change them, which inevitably meant a complete outfit swap, but it was also the right time of day to call Alistair and I hadn't done so in two days.

The Aurelia was on its way through the Panama Canal, heading for the western coast of America where we would catch up with it. The difference in time was now eight hours which meant if I hurried I would catch him as he rose, but before he left his cabin to find himself swamped in the tasks each new day brought.

There was another reason I was delaying my visit to the vicarage, though stalling might be a better word for it: I was becoming increasingly convinced the vicar might be guilty.

No alibi for the times of the murders, the embezzled money, his argument with Allen; reported by his own wife for goodness sake ... The list of evidence against him was getting longer every time I looked for something that worked in his favour. Even the slim hope that Beryl Forrester saw a woman had been dashed.

Felicity and Roy managed to turn up something new: a question about why Reverend David left his old parish to come to East Malling, but it felt innocuous, and I was stalling because I hoped Albert's visit to Dover might turn up something that would allow me to not go at all.

Poor Sadie had friends visiting, but I doubted they would stay – everyone has such busy lives. That meant she was probably alone, but would she think that preferable to having me turn up to quiz her again? Probably. I felt sure I would.

I needed to get back to the ship, that was the truth of it. The village where I grew up and knew most of the residents by name would always hold a special place in my heart, but at some point in the last few months it had stopped being home.

Perhaps it was as simple as my love for Alistair. He was so different from my ex-husband Charlie in so many ways: kindness, generosity, selflessness ... being the woman on his arm was a privilege not least because we were equals. With Charlie I had always been 'the old ball and chain'. With Alistair I was the woman he bragged to be dating. I got to do likewise and though we were many months into our relationship I was yet to shake the sense that I was ... how did Molly put it? Oh, yes, punching above my weight.

The boxing analogy summed it up nicely. Alistair was far too good for me, and I thanked the Lord that he didn't see things that way.

Ridiculously, my heart fluttered when the call connected at his end, and I heard his voice for the first time in forty-eight hours.

"Darling. How are you?"

Tea and Cake

"Two teas and a coffee, please," Albert requested of the lady behind the counter.

"And a slice of the chocolate cake," hissed Mindy.

"And a slice of chocolate cake," Albert added.

"Ooh, that sounds good," agreed Roy. "Make that two."

Albert rolled his eyes but said nothing. They were supposed to be surreptitiously enquiring about Reverend David Gentry, not filling their bellies. However, he noted that the chocolate cake did indeed look delicious and there was no good reason not to use the cake as a prop.

"Make that three pieces," he concluded.

"Doreen, two teas and a coffee, please," the lady said over her shoulder.

Both women wore dark green tabards to protect their clothes. They were in their very late sixties, possibly seventies though Albert always liked to give ladies the benefit of the doubt. One was called Doreen, he knew already, but they were not wearing name badges, so the other lady's name remained a mystery for now.

Were they the best people to ask, or would they get distracted serving others and not be able to give considered answers? Albert chose to ask an adjacent question first.

"We work for a local historical society," Albert lied. It was a ruse he'd employed before because it gave a reason for his desire to ask questions that might otherwise appear intrusive.

The lady serving the cake looked up.

"I wonder, do you know, are any of the people here," he angled his body back toward the tables and chairs behind them to show who he was talking about, "ones who have lived here a few years and are regular members of the church congregation?"

"Oh, ah," the lady peered around Albert, Mindy taking a sidestep to give her a better view of the room. "Well, you can ask that lady in the red coat." She dipped her head in the direction of a table set to the left. "That's my sister. She and I have been here forever," she laughed nervously after her claim. "Or you can ask me if you have questions."

"Why don't you take a short break, Sally?" suggested Doreen. "I've got this." She set down three steaming mugs, one distinctly darker than the other two. "Milk, sugar and sweetener are all over there," she nodded toward the far end of the counter where a small table held all the accompaniments a person might need.

Albert, Roy, and Mindy took their mugs and plates to the table, smiling at the lady in the red coat who looked up with questioning eyes at the three strangers choosing to sit with her in a room where less than half the tables were taken.

"They're with me," called Sally, allaying her sister's concerns before the strangers could take their seats.

"Well, hello then, I guess," she said, putting her phone down. "I'm Katie." She frowned at Albert, her brows knotting until she figured it out. "Hey, aren't you ..."

"Albert Smith?" Albert knew what she was going to say. "Yes, I am," he admitted. It changed the tack he had intended to take and had to reveal the truth to Sally now that she was coming to take a seat. "Sorry," he spoke as Katie's sister touched her chair to pull it out. "We're not really from a historical society. I'm Albert Smith."

Sally looked at her sister with a completely blank face.

Katie shook her head with a sorrowful expression. "How many times have I stressed the need to watch the news? Albert Smith is the one who saved all those people from that cave in Wales."

Sally's head snapped back to take in her unexpected celebrity visitor. "You don't say."

Before either lady could shoot off on a tangent, Albert jumped in quickly.

"The news made a bigger story of it than the truth deserved, but I'm afraid I have another matter I need to enquire about." Leaving that tantalising hook hanging in the air, both ladies bit.

"What is it?" asked Katie.

"Are you trying to solve another mystery?" Sally begged to know.

Roy clapped Albert on the back, taking attention away from his friend for a moment.

"That's exactly right, girls," he double pumped his eyebrows, ever the flirt. "Albert here is on the trail of a killer."

His remark caused wide eyes and a shared glance between the sisters. They believed Roy, but they had no idea how that could have anything to do with anything they might know.

Albert did his best to explain. "I'm sure you both recall Reverend David Gentry."

"Coo, yes," said Sally, cutting her eyes sideways at Katie. "My sister had ever such a crush on him."

"I did not!" Katie shot daggers from her eyes. "I merely said he was easy to look at and I only said that once."

"Katie never married," Sally felt there was a need to explain. "Instead she's been preying on the single men of the parish for the last forty years."

Katie's face was the colour of a beetroot, and her jaw muscles were bulging as she attempted to keep her wrath in check.

"In fact," Sally continued, "If either of you two are single, you might want to ..."

"One more word Sally," Katie warned.

Mindy leaned in close to Albert's ear. "Should we try to find someone else to talk to?"

Albert whispered back, "You go. I think I might have to keep these two apart."

Approximately a nanosecond after he said the words, Katie launched the dregs of her coffee mug at her sister. They splashed harmlessly over her dark green tabard.

Sally sniggered and that proved to be the last straw.

Katie, easily seventy years old, launched herself bodily at her sister, grabbing handfuls of hair on either side of her head.

Mindy was already on her feet, but backing away, not moving to intercept. The gentlemen could deal with this one.

Using the commotion as a reason to move tables, Mindy took her cake and coffee to a likely looking couple.

"Does this happen here often?" she asked, nudging a chair out with one foot. "Mind if I join you? I doubt my drink could survive staying where I was."

To accentuate her point, the sisters' table shunted a foot to the left spilling warm, brown liquid across the Formica surface.

Roy had Katie around the waist, his hands interlocked at the front though his battle to pull the enraged woman away from her sister wasn't going as planned.

Katie employed several words the audience were not used to hearing in the church hall, two of which caused a gasp from the woman sitting next to Mindy.

Albert did his best to coach Sally not to push her sister any further, but he was likewise wasting his time.

Sally was having a great time. "This is what you get for stealing my boyfriend, you slut."

Incensed, Katie struggled to get free of Roy's grip. "That was forty-eight years ago! And you were cheating on him with Ronnie Taylor!"

"I was not!"

Mindy turned away to face her tablemates.

"Hello, I'm Mindy."

She tried to get their attention, however the fight was proving all-consuming, and the entire room gave a collective sharp intake of breath when something hard connected with something less so.

Mindy twisted around to find Roy holding his nose. There was blood coming from between his fingers where Katie had just delivered a high elbow. It could have meant an escalation since Katie was once again free to launch a physical attack, but the sight of blood often proves to be a reality check and this occasion was no different.

"Oh, goodness. Are you all right?" Katie looked horrified. "I didn't mean to hit you that hard. I just wanted to kill my sister a little bit."

Choosing not to enquire what a little bit dead might look like, just in case Katie volunteered a demonstration, Albert asked, "Is there a first aid kit anywhere?"

Mindy watched until the foursome shuffled off to the kitchen area where Doreen was already fishing around to find the box of bandages. As the excitement settled, she turned her attention back to the couple at the table.

"Have you lived here long?" she asked.

The Unknown Element

Rex was feeling better by the time his human came back for him. The windows in the car were open an inch but that just meant the cold air was getting in and if he was going to be cold, Rex would rather be outside where he could wander around.

The headache was little more than a dull ache now though his neck still didn't feel right.

Buster bounced out of the car and down to the ground the moment Mindy opened it. Rex was a little more sedate in his exit, wanting to check his feet were going to support his body before he did anything more than stand in one spot.

"Feeling better?" Albert asked, ruffling the fur around Rex's neck.

Rex leaned into the old man's leg, returning the affection.

"Can you explain it again?" asked Roy, his voice rather nasal with a cotton ball stuffed up each nostril. He had a tinge of bruising around the bottom corner of each eye; a mark of battle he'd not worn since his early twenties and that was when a cricket ball slipped through his fingers not as the result of failing to duck someone's fist.

Mindy made sure Buster's lead was firmly clipped to his collar and checked to be sure Albert was ready to follow with Rex before setting off.

As she began to walk, she said, "The couple I talked to are Rosie and Jim. They remembered Reverend David right enough but couldn't tell me anything about why he left."

"That's about all we got too," Albert admitted. In between tending to Roy's face there had been time for him to slip in a few questions, though no worthwhile information came from it.

"Well, when Rosie and Jim couldn't tell me anything about the vicar directly, I asked about events that occurred around that time or just before he left."

"And you got something," Roy guessed, his voice hopeful.

Mindy nodded, looking back over her shoulder as she led the two pensioners away from the church.

"It might be nothing," she admitted, her tone close to apologetic, "and they argued about it, but Rosie told me someone ran over a little boy just weeks before the vicar left the parish."

"He killed a kid?" Albert didn't even try to keep the shock out of his voice.

Mindy was quick to correct him. "I never said he was killed, and Rose told me the vicar was right at the centre of the drive to help the family raise the money needed to have their house adapted. She remembered it because no one could understand why the vicar left right when the family needed him."

Albert felt his lips tighten. Terrible things happen to good people all the time; his service as a police officer taught him that better than most, but it still pained him to hear about children suffering.

"So what does this have to do with the vicar now?" Albert pressed.

Mindy shrugged. "Like I said, this could be nothing, but if he was spending a lot of time with one family, trying to help in their darkest hour only to up and move to another parish right without warning, maybe they will know something others don't."

As reasoning goes, Albert considered Mindy's to be sound.

"Is it far?" Roy asked.

Mindy checked her phone. She was using the maps app to find her way; a trick Albert had learned only recently with his own device.

"Just around the corner if Rosie had it right. She couldn't tell me the exact address but was certain they live in Turner Close."

They had to knock on three doors before they got an answer and a further five before they found someone who could give them the right door number for the Goodalls.

At two forty-three on a Monday afternoon, there was no way to guess if there would be anyone in, but the distant shadow behind the frosted door promised a result five seconds before the door opened.

A weary looking woman in her early thirties looked out at the strangers on her door.

Buster barked at her, *"Are you the killer?"*

Rex frowned. *"I don't think that is why we are here."*

"Oh."

Above the dogs, Mindy took the lead.

"Hello. Sorry to disturb you like this. We are looking for Abigail Goodall."

The woman's face twitched, one eyebrow hiking up her forehead. "That's me."

"Sorry, again," Mindy apologised. "We have some questions about Reverend David Gentry." Albert had coached her on what to say and how to make sure she didn't come across as aggressive or demanding – always apologise for taking up their precious time, he'd said, it puts them in a position of wanting to forgive you and that's the best way to get inside. Then you have to give them a reason to help you. "I'm afraid he's in a bit of bother and we're trying to help him."

"David's in trouble? What kind of trouble?"

It was educated guesswork that the vicar would be held in high esteem by the family he'd been helping, the hope being that claiming to be on his side would grease the wheels and get them past the door.

It worked too, Abigail volunteering to let them inside.

Glad to be out of the cold, they removed their shoes to pad after the lady of the house in their socks. She led them to her kitchen, where underfloor heating beneath the stone tiles made the floor wonderful to stand on.

An adapted chair sat to one side of the dining table.

"My Timmy's," she explained. "He was in an accident when he was four. Someone ran him over and drove off. Left him in the street. He shouldn't have been outside of course, that's my fault. I thought he was playing in the garden, but the side gate was open and he ..." she broke off what she was saying, the memory still painful after so many years. "Sorry, you don't need to hear all that. How can I help you?" she asked, forcing a smile onto her face. "What is it that you want to know? David's been wonderful to us, so if I can help I will do whatever I can. What sort of trouble is he in?"

"Wonderful how?" Albert asked, ignoring Abigail's question.

"Well," Abigail indicated the chair again. "He was here the day after it happened. Or rather, he came to find us in the hospital. He was there to give spiritual support of course, but also to ensure we received all the other help we would need. Timmy's spine was severed just beneath his shoulder blades, so his arms work, but they were both broken very badly ..." She trailed off again, her eyes unfocused to look at the past.

In a quiet voice, Albert said, "He made sure you were getting the assistance you would need to help Timmy come home and live as normal a life as possible."

Abigail lifted her head, swiping away a tear. "Yes. Like I said, he was wonderful. Timmy is at school right now. It's hard for him. It always will be, but he's my little ray of sunshine." She fought emotions clawing to get to the surface even as she shoved them back down.

"I need to ask about his move to another parish," Albert introduced the topic that brought them to Abigail's door. The vicar acted as a rock in the Goodall family's time of need, but that was what Albert expected of a parish priest. The job was more than just sermons, weddings, and christenings. Being responsible to the community was what the job really entailed in his opinion. "We believe he left here not long after Timmy's accident. That must have been hard for you."

"It was," Abigail admitted.

Arriving at the big, important question, Albert asked, "Do you know why he left your parish?"

Abigail didn't need to think about it. She required no time to consult her memory. She simply shook her head and said, "He told us the church needed to move him." Silence fell, Abigail's three guests pondering what that could actually mean when she added, "It didn't really matter though because he's never left *us*."

Albert felt his head tilt a little to the left to accompany the question forming on his face. "You still hear from him?"

"Every week," Abigail confirmed. "If it were not for him ... well, we certainly wouldn't have been able to afford Timmy's chair. Or his converted bedroom. That and the bathroom alone cost twenty-five thousand pounds."

Albert heard Roy repeat the number as a murmur while it bounced around inside his own skull.

"I need to be clear, Abigail. You are telling us that the Reverend David Gentry himself gave you twenty-five thousand pounds."

Abigail's brow knitted, confused by the question.

"Yes. And another ten thousand just this week because Timmy has outgrown his old wheelchair and goodness knows Max and me can't afford to replace it. Those motorised things are like buying cars."

There it was. The vicar hadn't embezzled the money to meet his own selfless desires; he'd been giving it away to a family to meet their desperate needs. It was a noble act, or would have been if it was his money. Instead, he took what was not his to give away and had been going without to repay it ever since.

It wasn't a clever thing to do, but in many ways that made it even more noble. Even more so when one took into account the man was now in jail refusing to divulge where the money had gone for fear someone might try to take it back.

Abigail had fallen quiet, silenced by the way her guests reacted, but only for a few moments. She began to ask why the money was so important, but Albert wasn't listening.

He needed to make a phone call.

Back at the Vicarage

- -

The clock ticked loudly, increasing its volume deliberately to remind me I was stalling. It had been two hours since I got home; long enough for Albert and co to make it to Dover and start asking questions. That they hadn't texted me with an update or any new information was indication enough that they were not getting anywhere.

We were working as a team and that meant I held a responsibility to do my part. Sure, it wasn't my job to solve this case, but when had that ever stopped me before?

I was alone in the house. Barbie and Hideki were out for the day and Jermaine had taken a car to the local Fortnum and Masons store. He needed ingredients and I had made it clear I wasn't planning to go anywhere before he got back. It was a good thing I hadn't promised though because I would be about to break it.

Jermaine insists on going more or less everywhere with me. He is my bodyguard as well as my butler and, to be fair, I do have a habit of getting into bother.

Regardless, I was heading to the vicarage where I was going to have to quiz Sadie once more. It bugged me that the vicar had no alibi for either murder. I knew from Albert that the vicar was at the church council meeting two nights ago, but where did he go from there? According to Sadie he didn't come home until after nine. That was the worst of it because it placed him at large when Beryl was killed.

Also the knife ...

The knife bothered me and thinking about it again set off an itch in the back of my skull. The knife was the single most damning piece of evidence. Quinn said it was the vicar's knife from his knife block in the vicarage. Finding it embedded in Allen Gibson's back with a set of the vicar's fingerprints attached was like a nail in the coffin, but there had to be something I could uncover.

Sadie believed her husband was guilty, and the only snippet of doubt turned up by our investigation so far was a question over why they came here in the first place.

It was all I had, so I was using it as an excuse to visit her again. I had questions about timings and alibis, but I wasn't holding out much hope.

I chose to walk despite the cold. It was only a half mile to the vicarage if I cut across the village and there was more than an hour of daylight left yet. I would be back before Jermaine even knew I'd gone out.

Leaving via the front door, I cut across the garden at an angle. There is an old stile in one of the outer fences that leads to a track through the woods. Barbie runs it with me sometimes, though not recently, the route taking a short, yet winding path through the woods to get to Baker Street.

I was just climbing down from the stile when my phone rang.

Fishing the device from my handbag I saw Albert's name displayed.

"We know what the money was for," he didn't bother with salutations.

I kept things equally brief, "Go on."

"The vicar was giving the money to the family of a kid in his old parish." I listened while Albert explained about a little boy called Timmy and his terrible injuries. It was a cruel fate, and one the vicar had clearly taken to heart.

By the time I came out of the trees and onto Baker Street I was armed with fresh purpose. Albert could have called the vicar's wife himself, but I agreed with his opinion that the questions were best asked in person.

Had Sadie known where the money went? She admitted they were always short each month, making it sound like they were barely making ends meet, but was she being convenient with the truth about the money her husband gave away and then had to repay to the church? I could imagine she would want to.

My prayers I would find the vicar's wife at home were rewarded. It was just after three and with the sky beginning to darken to the east, I saw the light come on inside the foyer of the vicarage a moment before the door opened.

"Patricia?" Sadie questioned, surprised to see me again so soon.

"Sadie. So sorry to be back at your door. There has been a development."

Sadie's eyes widened and she looked worried. "A development? I haven't heard anything. What is it? Have they released David?"

"Not yet, but maybe we can change that. Can I come in?"

Sadie glanced over my shoulder.

"Is it just you?"

I guess I do tend to travel with an entourage.

"Just me this time."

The vicar's wife stepped out of the way, welcoming me inside and shutting the door on the cold air outside. The temperature had dropped more than I'd expected, and I was genuinely cold. Below freezing doesn't happen all that often in the southeast corner of England where I live, and a thicker coat was called for.

"Come through to the kitchen," Sadie led the way. "I'm just making some dinner and there's no good letting it burn in the pan." She walked a few more steps, arriving at her kitchen where she asked over her shoulder, "So what is the development and how will it help to get my husband free?"

I didn't want to overdo it. We were a long way from proving the vicar innocent. At the moment it would be enough to shed some doubt on the charges against him.

"Timmy Goodall," I spoke the name of the injured child and watched to see if she would react.

"Who's that?" Sadie asked, her back to me while stirring a thick, rich ragu.

"A young boy who was injured in a hit and run incident just before David left his former parish to come here."

Sadie turned to check I was being serious. "That's terrible. Is he all right now?"

Poor Sadie. Her husband hid everything from her. She was so trusting.

Wanting to take her hand before delivering the truth I held back.

"Timmy's injuries are ones that will never heal. He needs continuous medical care and attention and specially adapted equipment so he can live as normal a life as possible." Sadie looked suitably aghast. "I'm afraid that's where the money your husband took has been going, Sadie."

Sadie shook her head slowly from side to side. "That is so like my David. Always putting everyone else first. He is such a generous spirit."

The back of my skull itched, and I turned my thoughts inward to consider what I might have just heard or seen.

Sadie turned back to her stove, stirring the pot of ragu again and lifting the wooden spatula to taste it.

"Needs oregano," she murmured to herself. Crossing the room, she opened the pantry door and went inside.

"Do you think we will be able to get the money back?" she asked, her voice echoing out from behind the door which had swung closed in her wake.

I blinked, processing her question but startled by it.

The pantry door opened again, the vicar's wife returning with a small glass jar in her right hand. Seeing the expression on my face, she paused in the doorway, and I couldn't stop my lips from what they needed to say.

"You said you couldn't hear what Allen Gibson and your husband were saying because they were inside the pantry."

"Yes, that's right," Sadie replied, her tone that of a challenge.

I bit my top lip nervously, my skull itching like crazy.

"Well, you were just in there and I could hear you perfectly."

Change of Direction

A lbert stared out of the car window. Rex was asleep, his body taking up seventy percent of the back seat and his head draped across Albert's left thigh. His jowls hung open and he was snoring lightly, one back leg twitching occasionally as he dreamed doggy dreams about squirrels or cats or giant hamburgers that wanted to eat him for all Albert knew.

Albert was yet to speak a word since they pulled away from the church carpark. Though the radio played and Roy chatted amiably with Mindy in the front of the car, Albert could not shift the feeling that he was missing something.

Since the very start, the vicar had seemed guilty, yet they were operating as if he were not and all the evidence against him was somehow fake. There was a term to be employed when this happened: framed.

In his years of police service, Albert only witnessed a suspect being framed twice that he could recall. It was rare and it never worked because the person attempting to construct the frame would always miss something.

They would fail to prevent the suspect from having a viable alibi – someone would have seen them or spoken to them on the phone at the time when they were supposedly committing their crime. Or the framer would forget a small detail that would expose them as the person behind it all.

Admittedly, had Albert ever been witness to a perfect frame, he would never have known about it. That was an awful thing to acknowledge, but miscarriages of justice did happen and he could only hope such a circumstance could not be linked to any of his cases.

However, looking at the vicar's case through the concept of a frame, who could stand to gain? Who would want to see him put away? What was he doing in Allen Gibson's house mere hours after his body was removed?

Pushing that last damning question to one side, for it made the vicar look guiltier than ever, Albert examined what he did know.

The vicar chose to selflessly give money to the family of an injured child.

Or did he?

Frowning, Albert spotted his assumption for what it was.

The vicar's wife told Patricia they were always short each month and now they knew why, but what had driven the vicar to such lengths. He embezzled money from a church roof fund to make Timmy Goodall's life more tenable, but if he was such a wonderful person, why did he leave the Kingsdown parish? Why did he up and move so soon after Timmy's accident.

"I need you to turn the car around."

Mindy cut her eyes to the rear-view mirror.

"We have to go back." There was no hint of discussion in Albert's tone.

Roy twisted in his seat to check on his friend.

"Everything all right, old boy? Did you leave something behind?"

Albert clenched his jaw, his brain working feverishly to join the dots.

They were on the road that led to the motorway and Mindy needed to change direction in the next two hundred yards or they would be heading north until the next junction occurred many miles later.

Ignoring Roy's questions, Albert thrust his head between the front seats and jabbed with his arm.

"Pull in!" he commanded. "Or take that sideroad so you can turn around."

Unsure what had changed, but motivated to do as the old man requested, Mindy flicked her indicator and let her right foot rise. The car slowed, but she wanted to know what was going on.

"What's happening, Albert? Why are we going back to the church in Kingsdown?"

"We're not."

Roy's eyebrows reached for the sky. "We're not? Then where are we going?"

"The archdeacon lied to us. I thought that maybe she was misinformed or had it wrong, but that's not it at all. She willingly chose to hide a secret and lied to protect it."

Mindy had one eye on her rear-view mirror. She wanted to perform a U-turn and watched to find a gap in the traffic that would allow it.

"What lie?" she asked. "What secret was she trying to protect?"

"That Reverend David Gentry ran down a four-year-old boy and drove away."

Anger descended across Mindy's vision. She met a lot of priests in her line of work and liked that she (almost) never caught them looking at her backside. They were supposed to be good people, but for the last two days she'd been working alongside folk who were trying to clear the name of a man who maimed a child, stole money, and probably murdered two people.

A gap in the steadily flowing traffic appeared. It wasn't anywhere near big enough, but Mindy floored her accelerator pedal anyway.

"Oh, I say!" Roy gripped the handle above his head and braced against the dash while thinking a third arm might be really useful.

Buster lost his footing, but stayed more or less in place, held there by Roy's legs.

On the backseat Rex lifted his head, his jowls on sideways to give his face a 'just ran hard into a wall' look.

"*Wassat?*" he asked, confused by the lurching car and conflicting forces acting upon his body.

The same forces pressed Albert's body into the corner of the seat where he held on for dear life amid a cacophony of horns.

Mindy's Mini powered across two lanes, the wheels spinning as they fought for traction. The backend slid out and back in, all four wheels coming into line facing one hundred and eighty degrees from where they had been just a second or so earlier, albeit one lane over.

With a large truck bearing down on her boot, Mindy took off like a scalded cat.

Now with a steely set to her brow, she asked, "Where am I going?"

In No Mood for a Discussion

- -

D over Cathedral dominates the skyline where it was built almost two hundred years ago. It is small as cathedrals go, but the focus of church matters for the region, nevertheless.

Mindy's wheels skidded to a stop as she entered the carpark, her passengers relieved to no longer be staring death in the face.

"Where did you learn to drive like that?" Roy asked, fighting to keep the quiver from his voice.

Mindy's answer came as she pulled into a parking space. "Grand Theft Auto on the PlayStation."

Albert's eyes roved the carpark, but not for long; the yellow Toyota Aygo was easy to spot.

Unless she had gone somewhere on foot, Archdeacon Janice Dock was somewhere on the premises.

Out of the car, Mindy noted Albert had Rex with him.

"You're taking the dog?"

"Yes. I've been lied to by a member of the clergy, ergo I no longer give a stuff about whatever rules they might have regarding my favourite companion." With that he started walking, determined strides making a beeline for the main entrance of a squat office building set separate to and away from the cathedral itself.

Roy went with him, the men leaving Mindy to grab Buster and hurry to catch up.

Inside, they were met with two sets of double doors, beyond which a receptionist at a desk set to one side looked up with a frown.

"Please leave your pets outside."

Albert fixed her with a look that was only a few notches shy of Superman's laser beam vision.

"No. The dogs come with us. I need to see Archdeacon Janice Dock right now. Bring her out here or I shall search the place for her."

Roy made a choking sound. He'd known his friend to be blunt and determined before, but this was a new level.

Even Albert recognised that he was acting differently to his usual calm, polite self. Had recent events changed him? Hounded by the police as he hunted a master criminal no one else would believe existed. Then hounded by the public and the press when he successfully proved he was right all along ... it made him see the world through a new lens.

He was done taking his time and being polite. People had been murdered and he wanted to confirm he was right about why.

"I beg your pardon," said the receptionist, rising indignantly to her feet. Vanessa Woodbridge rarely had to deal with anyone's rudeness, but she was not beyond ejecting the people now crowding her desk. She was most certainly not going to expose one of the archdeacons to them.

Albert assessed her reaction and chose his course of action. "Find her myself it is."

"You most certainly will not!" Vanessa exclaimed, starting to come around her desk.

Albert, however, had stopped listening. He was crouching next to Rex, one hand on his collar where he held the clip to his lead.

"Now, Rex, I know how clever you are, so please find the lady priest we met yesterday. Can you do that?"

Rex was so impressed by his human he gave him a lick to the chin.

"*You've grown so much.*" He wagged his tail. "*Of course I can find her.*" Turning to Buster, he remarked, "*See? Humans can be trained. He would never have thought to use my nose a few months ago. Now he understands where his weaknesses lay and how best to get the job done.*"

"I am calling the police!" Vanessa threatened, picking up her phone.

A voice from their left stayed her hand.

"That will not be necessary, Vanessa. Thank you."

Albert, Mindy, Roy, and both dogs swivelled to confirm the identity behind the new voice.

"Hello, again," said Archdeacon Janine Dock. "I saw you arrive and assumed it was me to whom you wished to speak."

"Is everything all right?" asked Vanessa, her face showing the doubt she felt.

The archdeacon looked her way. "Yes, Vanessa. Thank you for your concern." She said the words but nothing in her tone or body language suggested she believed what she was saying. Nevertheless, she shifted her gaze back to meet Albert's accusing eyes and said, "Please come with me. We can talk in private in my office."

Vanessa looked like she wanted to complain about the dog again, but she held her tongue and watched the procession depart down a wide corridor.

Olive Oil

S till occupying the door to the pantry, Sadie blinked. That she was lost for words was an understatement.

Now certain I had caught her in a lie, I pressed a little further. "You told me your husband and Allen were shouting. That was the reason you gave for why you didn't go in or open the door."

"Well, yes," Sadie started moving again, crossing the kitchen to get back to the pan of gently bubbling ragu. "I mean, I exaggerated a bit obviously. I heard what they both said, but I wasn't going to admit to the police that I heard my husband threaten Allen with violence. That wouldn't have done him any good, now would it?"

She was brushing my concerns away as though needless or insignificant; her dinner was more important.

Her dinner.

"That's a big pot of ragu," I remarked. "Who do you have coming to dinner?"

This time Sadie put the spatula down and faced me, impatience etched into her features.

"No one, thank you, Patricia. I am batch cooking, if you must know. That's not an uncommon habit."

It wasn't, but there was something very off about the whole picture and my skull wouldn't stop itching.

Sadie faced the stove again, picking up the spatula once more.

"You said you had something that was going to help my husband's case. Please tell me it wasn't that thing with the injured child. Finding out where the money went hardly works in his favour. He still embezzled it, didn't he? He still killed Allen to protect his secret and then poor old Mrs Forrester when she saw him leaving Allen's house." She paused to light the flame beneath a large saucepan and reached to her right to pick up a bottle of olive oil. Adding a glug to the water, she leaned one hip against the stove to pierce me with her blue eyes. "Do you have anything else? Or is that it?"

I stared at the bottle of olive oil. It was the same one in Beryl's kitchen, but did I believe she was the sort to splash out on top end ingredients? Honestly, I doubted Beryl Forrester had ever bought a bottle of olive oil in her life. It would class as fancy foreign muck in her books. She was a meat and two veg kind of woman and thinking back to the meal she looked to be preparing, olive oil ought to play no part in it.

Chief Inspector Quinn said the bottle had the vicar's fingerprints on it, which it would if it came from the vicar's house.

The itching in my skull shut off like someone flicking a switch. I knew the answer. I knew why the vicar had no alibi and why all the evidence pointed his way. I knew why his fingerprints were found at the crime scenes and why he was so sloppy as to leave the knife from his own kitchen in the back of his first victim.

He was set up.

Wanting to back up, but feeling my feet rooted to the spot, I asked, "How did you know the name of the second victim?"

Lies Exposed

I n the quiet of her office, Albert stared at the archdeacon.

"Well?" he encouraged her to start talking.

She retreated behind her desk, using it as a barrier though Albert knew it was more a mental one than physical. Facing the door, she had Albert, Roy, and Mindy silently waiting for the truth.

"I lied to you yesterday," she admitted.

As an opening line, it pleased Albert. He expected she might compound her previous lies with fresh ones intended to conceal the truth yet further.

When no one said anything, the trio of investigators letting the silence lubricate her jaw, the archdeacon slumped into her chair.

"I'm sorry, but those were my instructions. Orders, I guess you could call them."

"From whom?" Albert pushed, curious to learn how high the conspiracy went. "And don't say God, because I will get mightily upset if you do."

The archdeacon looked up, her face filled with disappointment.

"It doesn't matter who, Mr Smith. The truth was to be concealed, but I can see that is no longer possible. I hope that you can see how damaging this could be for the church. It does no good to anyone for the truth to be known. Do you think Timmy Goodall will benefit? Think of him."

"That's a low blow," Albert sneered. "I expected better. Tell me, was David Gentry drunk when he hit the child and drove off? Was that why he left the scene when any decent person would have stopped and taken their medicine? Is that why he embezzled the money? Guilt for his actions?"

The archdeacon tilted her head, an enquiring look playing across her face.

"You think David Gentry ran over the child?"

Albert twitched his eyes at Roy who gave a 'beats me' look in return.

If the vicar hadn't run over the kid and left him paraplegic, then who had?

Adding it all up

S adie's brow furrowed, confusion over my question gripping her.

"You told me you were being questioned by the police all day and that when I came to your door the first time you had not been in long at all. How did you know Beryl Forrester had been killed?"

Sadie shrugged, an exaggerated gesture where her shoulders came up to almost touch her ears.

"I guess I heard someone talking about it at the police station."

"You heard that a member of your husband's parish had been murdered, but you don't recall where or how you learned about it?" I was challenging her though goodness knows why. I could see she was the killer.

"I have had a few other things on my mind, you know!" Sadie snapped out the words, the last few coming like a whip being cracked.

"You were late to the church council meeting," I accused. "Mavis gave me a list of people who she talked to about what Beryl Forrester saw. You were one of them."

Sadie laughed. "And how long was that list? Mavis is a gossip without parallel. Tell her anything and the whole village knows within a few hours."

"That's true," I replied. "But how many of them have access to the vicar's fingerprints? How many of them had the chance to provide an alibi for him, but weren't able to even though they live in the same house? Who was late to the meeting the night Beryl was killed?"

Sadie's features took on a mocking expression. "Beryl was killed after the meeting. The time on her watch showed that as clear as anything. I was still talking to the church council members at the hall at eight-thirty when David killed her."

"How do you know what the time on her watch said?"

Sadie's face froze. I had her and she knew it. I needed my feet to move. I should have run out of her house five minutes ago when my brain finally supplied the right answer, but I hadn't.

"Clever," Sadie spat. "You can't prove anything though. It's David's fingerprints on the murder weapons and in their houses. He's the one who embezzled the money. He's the one who had the fight with Allen!"

"Did he?" I asked. "I think Allen was helping him. Allen could have brought the missing money to light at any point since he first discovered the discrepancy, assuming that is, that he wasn't complicit from the start. I think they were managing it between them, but you were fed up trying to make ends meet. You wanted David to stop, but rather than walk away and get divorced, you chose to frame him for murder."

"He made us poor!" she screeched. "He didn't have to give that family anything. No one knew. We could have just left, but he had to do the right thing. He always wanted to do the right thing. Well, I was fed up being poor. I want things. I want holidays and a nice car. I want to have money in my purse when I open it and when I threatened to leave, David said he would tell everyone what really happened!"

What a Man will do for Love

"The wife?" Albert could scarcely believe it.

The archdeacon sat back in her chair looking pleased with herself though Albert felt she had no right to any emotion other than shame.

"That is correct," she confirmed her previous statement. "Do you really believe the bishop would permit a priest to stay in office if he was responsible for a hit and run incident." It was a rhetorical question and got no response from any of the three people still staring at her. "David came to me in the days after the incident. He heard about the little boy and his terrible accident as did everyone else in the community. It was all over the news. What did not make the news was the state of David's car."

"You helped him to cover up a crime," Albert accused.

"And I cannot undo what is past, but his wife denied his accusations. On the night in question she had been out drinking. By herself, I believe. They were not yet married, but the date had been set and he was very much in love with her. She arrived at the vicarage here in Dover very much the worse for alcohol and went straight to bed if David's account of the events is to be believed. It was the following morning that he discovered the damage to his car. Sadie denied all knowledge of the incident or that she had even been in the area where the Goodalls live. He could have reported his suspicions to the police, but instead asked to be moved."

"Why?" Albert could not help but press for more information.

The archdeacon was forced to speculate. "I believe he suffered from a heavy heart. He knew his intended was to blame, but rather than break off the engagement, which he should have done, he went through with the marriage and did what he could to make amends to the boy and his family. However, staying in his parish was just one step too far for him. He didn't exactly want to move, but he felt there was no better option. I arranged the transfer myself, keeping it quiet and placing him in a parish with an ageing vicar who was due to retire."

Albert believed what he was hearing, yet struggled to believe the archdeacon knew the truth and did nothing with it. "When did you learn of this?"

"More than a year after the event. David sought me out. I was his mentor; the priest assigned to guide and help him through his early years. When he first requested the transfer and begged my assistance, I gave it willingly, but asked why the urgency. That was when he claimed he was doing it for his intended, so she could be near to her family."

Albert narrowed his eyes at the archdeacon, and she looked away.

"I apologise for lying to you. It was ... I believed it was for the best to repeat the lie David told me. As I said, it was more than a year after his move to East Malling when he came to me to admit what he had done and to assure me the money he'd taken from his parish church roof fund would all be replaced. He had no proof, you see? He believes his wife ran that little boy over and left the scene because she knew what would happen to her if she stayed and was found to be under the influence. He believes," she repeated, "but belief is all we have. There is no proof."

Albert reached for his phone. "I wouldn't be too sure of that. Patricia Fisher is more than likely interviewing Sadie Gentry as we speak. If the vicar did all that just to make amends for a crime his wife committed, there is no chance he killed Allen Gibson or Beryl Forrester."

Roy and Mindy gasped. Staring right at each other, they said, "The wife did it!"

Knife-wielding Maniac

My phone rang. The familiar ringtone came from inside my handbag, hanging next to my jacket on the back of a chair at the kitchen table. The kitchen table that was on the other side of Sadie.

The sound punctuated the tension in the room to act as a catalyst to get things moving. Sadie launched toward the stove, the simmering pan of ragu becoming a boiling hot missile heading for my face a heartbeat later.

I ducked it, but coming back to upright I caught a flash of light on a shiny surface – the vicar's wife was coming for me with a knife!

Someone screamed, my brain needing a moment to realise it was me making the high-pitched noise.

Sadie swiped the air, the blade cleaving the space in front of my face in two without touching my skin. She hadn't missed on purpose though; the knife missed because I was toppling backwards.

Twisting, I got a hand down to the kitchen tile, the only thing that stopped me from landing flat on my back. I knew for sure that I either got away from her right now or she was going to claim her third victim. Falling to the floor would mean curtains, so with a grunt of effort I threw myself toward the kitchen door.

"Jermaine!" I wailed. The text I sent him was ages ago. Was he outside waiting for me to exit the property, too polite to come knocking? The wonderful man had saved my life so many times in the past, surely he could do so one more time.

He wasn't here right now though and that meant I was going to have to fend for myself.

Sadie had put everything into her first murderous swing of the knife and missing meant her inertia pulled her off balance. It was that and only that which allowed me to get a few feet between us. Wailing like I was being chased by a knife-wielding maniac (because I was), I ran through the house.

I got to the front door and yanked it open only for the safety chain I failed to spot to halt my escape. Still racing forward, I almost ran into it with my face in my haste to get out. Fiddling with the chain, my fingers too nervous to operate it, I screamed again when the knife thunked into the door two inches in front of my eyes.

Sadie's throw missed my head, but only through luck on my part.

Snarling her rage, she ran at me and I jumped backward, falling through the door leading to her lounge.

This time I wasn't able to get a hand under my body, sprawling across the carpet on my back in time to see Sadie grip the knife to wrench it from the front door.

I kicked the lounge door shut, rolling onto my feet as fast as I could possibly move so I could throw my weight against it. I needed to get back to the kitchen and the back door. Or I had to go out of a window. I was on the ground floor after all, but I couldn't move away from the door I now held shut with my body because Sadie would come through it the instant I did.

To accentuate that point, she threw herself at the other side, rocking me back a few inches. Her fingers appeared around the frame only to be snatched back again amidst a torrent of expletives when I shoved my shoulder against the frame to squish them.

Looking around for something I could use, I hoped I could block the door with a piece of handy furniture. In a movie there would be a grandfather clock or a bookshelf I could topple. Here there was nothing.

That thought went out of my head when Sadie picked a new tactic and drove the knife right through the door. Yet again, it missed my face by no more than an inch or two and scared the living daylights out of me.

"I'm going to kill you, Patricia Fisher!" she screamed through the hole the knife made, pulling it out to drive it through again. The second strike almost caught my hip and I had to change my position to brace the door with just my hands while praying she wouldn't guess where my flesh was.

It was literally the worst game of battleships ever played and I didn't get to take a turn at all.

When the knife plunged through the thin wood for a third time and then a fourth, I accepted my strategy possessed a limited lifespan.

My breath coming in terrified, heaving lumps, I waited for the fifth strike, and when the knife came through the wood, I wrenched the door open.

The knife came with it, ripping it from Sadie's grip. For a frozen second we faced each other. She is taller, heavier, twenty-five years younger, and probably stronger than me. Also, I have no fighting skills and I was too terrified to throw a punch even if I wanted to.

However, a shadow outside the front door, one Sadie couldn't see because she was facing me, gave me the boost of hope I needed.

Screaming, "Jermaine!" at the top of my lungs, I swung an awkward kick at Sadie's shins and legged it in the opposite direction.

The kick landed, but I was moving too fast in the opposite direction to see whether it had any real effect. Clearly, it didn't do much, the sound of the knife being ripped back out of the door enough to convince me Sadie was right on my heels again.

I ran through the door at the other end of the living room, smashing it to one side with my shoulder. Now in the dining room that opened into the kitchen, I could see I was going to make it to the back door. Now I just had to pray it wasn't locked.

Paul Walker

- -

A lbert, Roy, Mindy and the dogs raced from the church offices, Mindy's younger legs getting her to the car first.

"*This is so exciting!*" barked Buster. "*Any idea what the heck is going on?*"

Rex barked back, "*I think my human just worked out that the vicar isn't the killer.*"

"*Oh, cool.*" Buster's face went thoughtful. "*Who is then?*"

"*Beats me, but they seem awfully excited about it.*"

Albert tried Patricia's phone for the fifth time, not liking one bit that she wasn't picking up. When she failed to answer yet again, he abandoned the direct strategy for one that might yield a different result.

"Hello, Mindy," Felicity answered her phone. She had a pair of reading glasses balanced on the end of her nose, necessary for the task at hand. "I'm in the middle of ..."

She didn't get to complete her sentence because Albert started talking. Fast.

"Felicity, it's Albert! I'm in the car with Mindy!"

"Goodness. Is everything okay?" The urgency in Albert's voice was enough to make her forget the very important, intricate, and detailed task she was performing.

"Yes and no," Albert snapped his reply. Mindy had the car in reverse, rocketing backward out of her parking space with Vanessa scowling at them from the building's front door.

"Hold onto something!" she yelled, yanking the handbrake and cranking the steering wheel to throw the front end around."

"More *Grand Theft Auto* moves?" Roy enquired, his spine compressing.

"Nah, that one's straight out of *Fast and Furious*. Gotta love Paul Walker."

Neither Roy nor Albert had any clue what their teenage companion was talking about and there was no time to enquire.

Albert waited for the gravity to change direction and when the Mini burned about a tyre's worth of rubber taking off down the road, he got back to his conversation with Felicity.

"Sorry, I've got your niece's phone. I don't have your number. We need you to get to East Malling. Where are you now?"

"At home."

Albert had no idea where that was; he didn't know Felicity Philips all that well and the subject had never come up.

Skipping forward in a bid to get to the end of the conversation, he said, "How soon can you get to the vicarage in East Malling? I think Patricia is there and she might be in real trouble."

Once Felicity assured him she was moving – on her way out of the house and getting into the car, he filled her in on a few more of the details. It was simple really. If one ruled out the vicar killing Allen and Beryl, the lineup of damning evidence could only provide one conclusion: his wife did it.

Albert couldn't yet figure out why she was framing her husband for two murders that appeared to have nothing to do with a secret almost no one else on the planet knew, but it was clear to him it had to be the case.

Ending the call with Felicity – she needed to concentrate on breaking the speed limit without crashing, endangering anyone else, or getting caught – he dialled three nines to report the crime he believed to be in progress.

That task complete, he asked if anyone had a number for Patricia's butler.

Trapped

The handle for the backdoor turned, but throwing myself at it and expecting to sail through when it opened, I merely bounced off. My shoulder fired pain messages back to my brain and my feet tangled, spilling me to the tile.

I was back where I found myself right after Sadie launched the pan of ragu at my head only now I had nowhere to go and at the far end of the kitchen, the only way out was back through the crazed murderer.

"It opens inward!" cackled Sadie, advancing on me, the knife held in front of her body. "If you are thinking of blaming me for your death, you can think again," she sneered. "You brought this on yourself. David was willing to go to jail for me. That's how stupid he is. He was worried they would force the Goodalls to give back the money. They never deserved it. What was that stupid kid doing in the street in the first place?"

"How can you think like that?" I scooted across the floor, trying to keep some distance between us. "You ran down a little boy. You changed his life forever."

"It wasn't my fault!" Sadie barked. "And David shouldn't have given them money he didn't have. He shouldn't have given them anything. There was no reason to. He made us poor. Do you know what that's like? I've been poor my whole life."

"There's no way you can get away with this, Sadie," I tried to sow some doubt, hoping I could make her pause long enough for Jermaine to rescue me. I didn't know for certain it was his shadow I saw outside the front door, but I was willing to bet it had been. Right now he would be making his way around the house to find me. He must have heard me screaming.

"I have gotten away with it, stupid. David is already in custody. All the evidence points to him. Even if he comes clean about the money and the Goodalls, what good do you think that will do him?"

With a deep breath to calm the tremor in my voice, I asked, "How will you explain my death?"

Sadie stopped moving. She hadn't thought of that.

"You won't be able to blame David," I pointed out.

A shadow fell across the kitchen window. Someone was outside. I just had to stall for a little longer. Jermaine would kick the kitchen door clean off its hinges, bursting into the room like the giant Jamaican ninja I knew him to be.

Sadie saw the truth in my words and the problem it created. However, she shrugged and raised the knife once more.

"I guess I'll have to get inventive. It's not like I can let you live, is it?"

I found myself saying, "No, I guess not," my attention focused not on the madwoman coming to gut me, but on the door behind her which had just opened.

Tracking my gaze, Sadie sniggered, "Really? The old, 'look behind you' trick?" She was about to say something else when the cool air hit her skin and she turned, spinning around to face the new threat.

I hadn't said a word because the person now standing behind Sadie was the last person I expected to see. Worse than that, I couldn't imagine how their appearance was going to improve my situation. Screaming at myself to get moving – I had the distraction I needed, if I was going to survive, I needed to clobber Sadie right now – I was just coming to my feet when the newcomer surprised me.

Mavis hitched up her skirt, gripping the material just above her knees and twisting sideways to lash out with a foot that came upward at an acute angle. It caught Sadie under her chin, snapping the young woman's head back with a crunch that turned my stomach.

Her head flopped back to its original position, her body unmoved from the spot it occupied, and I thought she was going to lift the knife so she could attack until it fell from her fingers to clatter on the floor.

Sadie remained upright for another second before dropping to her knees and crashing forward onto the tile, her head bouncing off the floor from the unchallenged impact.

Mavis still had one leg in the air, the knee folded back ready to deliver another strike. Watching Sadie crumple into a heap, she twisted her body and lowered the leg to join the other.

"It was the vicar's wife then?" she looked at me to supply an answer I figured she must already know.

Her words in the silence were like a pin to my bubble. I gasped in a breath of air, unaware I hadn't thought to breathe in the last thirty seconds.

"Oh, my goodness, Mavis," I rubbed my temples.

A small groan came from Sadie and that was enough to galvanise us both into action. I kicked the knife away, sending it across the room where it vanished underneath the refrigerator. It could be retrieved from there later.

Mavis fished out her phone. "Shall I call the police?"

"Yes, please." I found my own phone, whereupon I saw the missed calls from Albert and then Felicity. Given how many times they had called in the last ten minutes, I confidently concluded they had figured it out too. They could tell me how later. Right now I needed to call Jermaine.

The question of why he hadn't come looking for me was answered instantly – the stupid text hadn't sent. It was still sitting in my messages waiting for me to press the button.

Sighing, I called him. He would not be happy with me.

Aftermath

With Jermaine on the way, most likely running through trees and other obstacles rather than going around them in his haste, I felt myself sag. The terror left my body, washing out of my bloodstream and taking my energy with it.

I found one of the kitchen table chairs, dropping heavily into it. I was spent, but I did have some questions.

"Mavis," I spoke her name to get her attention. She was standing over Sadie still, keeping watch in case she came around.

The post office manager flicked her eyes in my direction. "Hmmm?"

"How did you do that?"

"What?"

"The kick thing. You swivelled on one foot and kicked an armed woman in the face like Jackie Chan. How did you do that? Aren't you sixty something?"

"Seventy-one, thank you very much," Mavis grumbled. "And I can feel every last one of those years in my hips."

"You didn't answer my question," I pointed out.

"Oh, that's just karate. I started doing classes back in the seventies."

"How come I don't know that? Does anyone know you are Jackie Chan's English sister?"

Mavis cast her eyes to the ceiling, consulting her memory. "Um, no, I don't think so. No one from the village anyway."

Okay, so mystery solved on the post office manager's unexpected ability to dispense violence. There was another question lined up behind that one though.

"What brought you to the vicarage today, Mavis?"

"Ah," she said. "Well, you remember when I said I told lots of people about what Beryl told me."

"Yes."

"I have been thinking about that list of names ever since, racking my brains to figure out if there was anything to it, if anyone stood out from the others."

"And the vicar's wife did?"

"Yes, but only in retrospect. I probably wouldn't have thought about it at all except she came by the store earlier today and she bought olive oil. I might have thought nothing of it, but she only bought a bottle last week, so she either dropped that one … or she left it at Beryl's house. Also, only about six people in the village buy that brand of olive oil and Beryl was never one of them."

I guess that sort of made sense. "But couldn't it have been the vicar who used it or dropped it or something?"

"Ah," said Mavis. "That might be a natural conclusion to reach, but I have it on good authority that the vicar never cooks. In fact, I believe he simply can't cook. His wife has moaned about it more than once in my presence. Anyway, going back to what I was saying about what Beryl said. When I told the vicar's wife, and said that Beryl saw a woman leaving Allen's house, she wanted to know how sure Beryl was that it wasn't just a small man."

Sadie gave herself away, asking a question no one else, not even me, had thought of.

I had one final question. "If you believed the vicar's wife might be the killer, why did you come to her house, Mavis?"

"To find you?"

I showed my confusion. How had she known to come here when I hadn't told anyone this was where I was going. I even failed to tell my butler.

"Kevin Munroe spotted you being let in. He was in the post office when I told Sharon I was leaving to tell you what I had figured out. I came straight here and heard you screaming."

"And you didn't call the police first?"

"Nah."

That appeared to be all she had to say on the matter and further conversation was cut off by the sound of someone yelling my name.

I frowned, recognising the voice, and lifted myself up from the chair to look through the dining room where I could see the front garden beyond the window.

"Patricia!" Felicity yelled my name again. "Patricia are you in there? I've called the police. They are already on their way? "Are you okay in there?" She started to hammer on the door and sticking her fingers through the letter box so she could more effectively shout my name into the house.

I let her in.

"Oh." She looked surprised to see me in one piece. "Albert made me think you were being chased by a knife-wielding maniac."

A tired snort escaped me, and I stepped back to show her the door into the next room where a large, knife-shaped hole let the light through.

"I was. Come on through. I know where the vicar's wife keeps her gin and I do not feel inclined to ask her permission."

We trekked through the house to find Mavis already at the drinks' cabinet. In the distance outside, the sound of sirens filled the air.

Leaving the Country

T wo days later I learned that the vicar was back. Albert called to let me know having heard it from Roy who was told by his wife. The church council were meeting daily at this point, and it made me glad I was no longer a member.

Reverend David would not be returning to minister to the parish. His time here was done. A new vicar would be appointed, the third in just a few years and I hoped whoever was next in line stayed around for a while.

Sadie wasn't coming back either, not for a few decades at least. Maybe she would get out of jail one day, but remanded in custody until her trial date came around, I doubted she would see freedom for a long time.

In the end it had all been about money. Her husband put them into debt to amend for her mistakes and she somehow blamed him for their financial situation.

With Albert on the line, I let him know I would be leaving the village the following morning. It was later than intended, but we would arrive in California in time to meet the Aurelia before it sailed.

"Me too," he replied. "I need to get away. Everyone recognises me here and it's driving me nuts."

I understood the sentiment. It wasn't too bad for me. I was on a luxury cruise ship most of the time where there were far bigger celebrities than me to spot.

"Where will you go?" I asked him. "Another culinary tour of the UK?"

"No, I think I shall go a little further afield this time. Did you see the news article about the Danish sceptre that was stolen a few weeks ago?"

"Yes." I remembered reading the article but hadn't thought about it since.

"Well, I think I shall look into that."

"You're going to Denmark? It's kinda cold there this time of year, Albert. Will Rex be okay at those temperatures?" Really I was challenging Albert, not Rex. Had he thought how the freezing air might affect his health?

Albert laughed a little, his deep rumble coming down the phone line. "I'll be taking a meandering route to get there, Patricia. It will be warmer by the time I arrive."

"Oh." I wasn't sure what else to say to that, so I wished him good luck and bade him farewell.

Barbie bounced into the kitchen.

"Hey, Patty, we're all packed. Are you looking forward to getting back to the ship?"

Hideki strolled in behind his girlfriend. "I, for one, would be happy to stay here a few more weeks. I love my job, but I'm in no desperate rush to get back to old people drinking too much champagne and passing out in the sun."

My feelings fell somewhere between the two. A few days ago the only thing I wanted was to get back to the ship, my suite, Alistair, and my dogs, not necessarily in that order. Now though, having been back in England for almost a week, I knew I was going to miss it.

England has a smell that will always be with me. It smells like home. Also, I knew that while I could stay on the Aurelia and in my job as the ship's detective for many years, there was an eventuality to coming home.

Alistair would hit mandatory retirement at sixty and he was already older than me. At some point, the globetrotting lifestyle would have to come to an end.

Then there was my surprising relative. I wanted to know more about her. I wanted to visit where she lived, and I absolutely had to read her journals. I could do some of that on board the Aurelia on the other side of the planet, but not all.

However, no matter what tied me to my home country, my flight was booked, and I was leaving the country in the morning. Gazing out of the kitchen window at the frost-laden garden beyond, I wondered what adventures might await me this time.

The End

Author's Notes:

H ello, Dear Reader,

Thank you for making it all the way to the end and beyond to find my random ramblings. It is a cold day in January as I write this final note. The snow is due to fall tomorrow and though I would normally welcome it, because we get snow so rarely in this part of the world and I have young kids for whom the cold white stuff is a fantasy come true, on this occasion I would rather it fell somewhere else. I have builders erecting a large extension on the back of my house and they need to put the roof on. That's not something they can do in the snow.

In this story I mention receiving a letter from the monarch on the occasion of one's hundredth birthday. If you are not British, you may not know about this practice. I do not know when it started but it has been a thing for as long as I can remember.

I also mention the Bisto Kids. They come from a long-running series of television advertisements in which two children follow the smell of Bisto (a brand name) gravy to its source at their mother's table.

HP sauce. The HP stands for Houses of Parliament which appear in the picture on the label. I'm fairly sure politicians had nothing to do with its creation nor its subsequent sale. Had they done so, the bottle would still be getting designed by a team of experts at a cost of several billion to the taxpayer and the ingredients would be voted on by a referendum that would produce an indecisive result and be argued by the opposition.

Ignoring the label, it is a fruit based brown sauce which some love and others hate. I am firmly in the latter camp.

The more observant readers might have spotted the name Beatrix Crawford and wonder where they had read it before. She appears in No Place Like Home, the tenth outing for Patricia Fisher, as the landlady of a B&B where Patricia initially stays when she arrives back in East Malling and refuses to move back in with her cheating, dirtbag husband, Charlie.

You may be wondering why I introduced Sylvia Dark, Patricia's distant and long-dead relative. Especially since I then did so little with the distracting back story. The reason is simple enough: I think I might like to write some period mysteries. Taking things all the way back to the 1920's when technology didn't rule the day has enormous appeal.

At this point, it is nothing more than a concept to be explored and there exists a danger I will never find the time. However, if I am going to write it, I want it to be a spin-off from Patricia's books. I guess the message from me is to keep your eyes peeled for announcements to follow.

I need to get this book edited and published so I can send Patricia and her friends back to the ship. She is about to meet her next nemesis, a former high-end thief coming out of retirement to test his mettle against a world-famous sleuth.

It's not just Patricia though, I have other series begging to be continued and I cannot wait to tell their tales.

Take care.

Steve Higgs

What's next for Patricia?

When someone takes a pot shot at a politician on board the Aurelia, Patricia has no sense of the mayhem heading her way.

The bullet missed its target, hitting an innocent bystander instead, but jumping into the investigation with both feet, Patricia and friends soon question if things are what they seem to be.

The politician is none other than the beleaguered Prime Minister of European state, Molvano, a man who insists the attempted assassination came at the hands of his opposition leader. It is an election year and what better way to clear the route to power than removing the person in your way?

If that is true, more attempts can be expected. Of course, a politician in danger isn't her only concern. There are bounty hunters on board searching for a convict on the run and a gang of thieves swiping debit cards.

It all adds up to a busy time for our favourite English sleuth, but when she uncovers the lies will she be the one in the assassin's crosshairs?

Free Books and More

Want to see what else I have written? Go to my website.

https://stevehiggsbooks.com/

Or sign up to my newsletter where you will get sneak peeks, exclusive giveaways, behind the scenes content, and more. Plus, you'll be notified of Fan Pricing events when they occur and get exclusive offers from other authors because all UF writers are automatically friends.

Click the link or copy it carefully into your web browser.

https://stevehiggsbooks.com/newsletter/

Prefer social media? Join my thriving Facebook community.

Want to join the inner circle where you can keep up to date with everything? This is a free group on Facebook where you can hang out with likeminded individuals and enjoy discussing my books. There is cake too (but only if you bring it).

https://www.facebook.com/groups/1151907108277718

Printed in Great Britain
by Amazon